TOUGH LIFE

Over breakfast, Brandon tried to explain that spending the day at the Beverly Hills Beach Club was not exactly a vacation for the hired help.

"I'm the first one there in the morning, and usually the last one to leave at night. And I'm so busy the rest of the time, I know I'm at the beach only because of sand collecting in my shoes."

Mr. Walsh speared a chunk of pineapple with a fork. He said, "TANSTAAFL, Brandon. There ain't no such thing as a free lunch. You get what you pay for in this world."

Brandon attempted to look alert for the sake of his argument. "But if you'd pay, let's say, half of what the car would cost, I could quit now and actually pretend it's summer."

Don't miss these books in the exciting
BEVERLY HILLS, 90210 series

Beverly Hills, 90210

Beverly Hills, 90210—Exposed!

Beverly Hills, 90210—No Secrets

Published by
HARPERPAPERBACKS

BEVERLY 90210 HILLS

SPELLING ENT. INC.

WHICH WAY TO THE BEACH?

A novel by Mel Gilden from teleplays by Charles
Rosin, Steve Wasserman & Jessica Klein, and
Jonathan Roberts

Based on the television series created by
Darren Star

HarperPaperbacks
A Division of HarperCollinsPublishers

This is a work of fiction. The characters, incidents, and dialogues are products of the author's imagination and are not to be construed as real. Any resemblance to actual events or persons, living or dead, is entirely coincidental.

HarperPaperbacks   *A Division of* HarperCollins*Publishers*
10 East 53rd Street, New York, N.Y. 10022

Copyright © 1992 by Torand, a Spelling Entertainment Company

Cover photos by Andrew Semel
Insert photos by Andrew Semel and Timothy White

First printing: June 1992

Printed in the United States of America

HarperPaperbacks and colophon are trademarks of HarperCollins*Publishers*

❖ 10 9 8 7 6 5 4 3 2 1

Contents

1

Billions of towels

BRANDON WALSH DOZED ON THE LONG
bus ride from Beverly Hills to the beach. He was
tired because it was summer, and he found going
to bed a little difficult. When the sun went down
sometime after eight, the air cooled just enough
to feel silky against his skin. Merely breathing
was an intoxicating experience. (*Intoxicating*,
while descriptive, was perhaps a bad choice of
words.) Going to a movie, hanging out, playing
basketball till midnight seemed not only natural,
but necessary for his teenage well-being.
Morning seemed years away. In Minnesota, not
even summer was ever this good.

But when it came, 5:30 in the (you should pardon the expression) A.M. arrived with the inevitability of final exams. No matter that it was summer and everybody you knew was strictly on R-and-R. No matter that the sun itself was not yet up. No matter that you were right in the middle of a bitchin' dream.

Brandon had been dreaming about the perfect beach, the perfect girl. She was tall and blond and without the taint of inhibition. She strolled along the beach toward Brandon. The wispy party dress she wore billowed around her, and was sometimes pushed tight against her body by the wind. In one hand she carried pumps that matched her dress and the breaking waves.

"I want you, Brandon. I need you."

That was all right with Brandon, but he remained cool. In his dreams, he was always able to remain cool.

While slouching in the bus seat with his arms crossed and his eyes closed, Brandon tried recapturing the moment the perfect girl lifted her arms to embrace him. But the shock of Brandon's father shaking him awake was too strong. The express bus—the very bus he was on—left for the beach at 6:30, and missing it was unthinkable.

Of course if he hadn't been such a jerk, if he hadn't totaled his car, Mondale, while drunk out of his gourd, he could have driven to the beach on his own schedule instead of the bus's. If he hadn't totaled Mondale, he wouldn't be working this summer at all. Yeah, *intoxication* was a very bad choice of words indeed.

Still, it would have been nice if his dad hadn't been such a stickler for building character. Over breakfast, Brandon tried to explain that spending the day at the Beverly Hills Beach Club was not exactly a vacation for the hired help.

"I'm the first one there in the morning, and usually the last one to leave at night. And I'm so busy the rest of the time, I know I'm at the beach only because of sand collecting in my shoes."

Mr. Walsh speared a chunk of pineapple with a fork. He said, "TANSTAAFL, Brandon. There ain't no such thing as a free lunch. You get what you pay for in this world."

Brandon attempted to look alert for the sake of his argument. "But if you'd pay, let's say, half of what the car would cost, I could quit now and actually pretend it's summer." Brandon had his eye on a Mustang, a vintage '65 'stang. Very cherry. The guy at the lot had promised to hold it till the end of summer. Despite how much he wanted it, Brandon was not convinced that giving up his entire summer for a car would make him a better human being, or even a better driver.

He failed to score. Mr. Walsh expressed the hope that Brandon have a nice day, and left for work.

Brandon had to walk a few blocks from the bus stop to the beach club. The sun was up and its light was already playing catch with the waves. The air was pleasantly warm. Eager kids were already migrating toward the beach with towels, foam boogie boards, and radios. It would be another scorcher.

In the employees' locker room, Brandon changed into his official green and white Beverly Hills Beach Club uniform. Very fancy. It even had his name squiggled in red over his breast pocket. The room was heavy with the smell of yesterday's sweat socks, and Brandon lifted a window to let in fresher air.

He looked out on the tanning deck and the beach beyond. His professional eye told him that many of the deck chairs were out of place and that not one of them was accompanied by a towel. Well, that's why he was here. Brandon sighed.

A well-built guy with curly blond hair was crossing the deck, apparently on his way to the volleyball courts. He was dressed for the day in a pair of def jams and sandals.

Brandon smiled and called down to him in a snooty voice, "Excuse me! Excuse me, young man!"

The guy glared over his shoulder at Brandon.

Brandon said, "I'm sorry but you'll have to leave. The beach club doesn't open for another fifteen minutes."

"In that case, *boy*, you can bring me a towel while I'm waiting." He grinned.

Brandon shook his head and laughed. The guy was impossible. Of course, impossibility was one of Steve Sanders' trademarks. He'd been called everything from cute and funny to a real jerk. Sometimes by the same people within minutes of each other. Brandon liked him, but was careful not to get caught up in Steve's schemes. "Up early this morning, man."

"The early bird catches the wormette," Steve said as he gestured toward the volleyball court with his head.

On one court, some guy Brandon didn't know was lobbing the ball around with a fantastic summer blonde wearing a bikini that covered the essentials without obstructing the view.

"She's with a guy, Steve."

"But not the right guy. Don't work too hard." Steve saluted Brandon and leaped over a deck chair on his way to the volleyball courts.

Brandon started putting out towels, and by the time he was finished, no more than two deck chairs in the entire place were still empty.

The volleyball courts were jumping—Steve was in there playing with the best of them—and a lot of paddle tennis was happening. Usually, people were polite to Brandon if they noticed him at all. Mostly, he was invisible, just one more appurtenance present for their comfort, like a towel or a beach umbrella.

On one paddle tennis court, a real battle was going on. Two middle-aged guys were obviously out for blood. One was fit and tanned, the other less so. Each of them had their partisans in the crowd. The guy who was in better shape was something of a loudmouth, always trying to psych out his opponent. Still, the action was fast and furious. They seemed to be about evenly matched. Brandon took his time putting out towels so he could watch awhile longer.

The loudmouth hit a tremendous slam at the outside corner and his opponent cried, "Out!"

They faced each other breathing hard, sweat dripping down their faces as if it were rain.

"Come on. That caught the line."

"Let's take it over, Rattinger."

Rattinger became excited. He said, "How could you not see it?" and opened his hands at the sky.

"I didn't see it."

"How could you not see it?"

"I saw it," Brandon said. In the sudden

silence, everybody looked at him: the specta-
tors, the two players, the immediate universe,
they all looked at him. He didn't know what sui-
cidal impulse had forced him to speak up. But
once the words were out, he wasn't sorry. He
had seen it. He only hoped the losing member
wouldn't be too hard on him.

Rattinger studied Brandon and said to the
crowd, "All right. Whatever the kid says goes.
Okay? That's fair, right, Edgar?"

Edgar wasn't happy about what was going
on, but he nodded. "So, nu?" he said.

"Mr. Rattinger's point," Brandon said.

Rattinger made victory noises and pumped
his arm. He acted like the king of England as he
walked off the court to small applause. "Game's
over. Thank you. Thank you very much." As he
passed Brandon, for the entertainment of the
masses, he said, "The envelope with the twen-
ties will be waiting for you at the front desk."
They both laughed at that. The guy was outra-
geous—Steve Sanders as an adult.

"Excuse me," asked Brandon, "but are you
Jerry Rattinger, the sports promoter?"

"Guilty as charged," Rattinger said good-
naturedly.

"I think you know my father, Jim Walsh."

"Jim Walsh is your old man?" The idea
astonished and pleased him. "I hear he's thinking about joining the club."

"Yeah!" Never before had this sounded to Brandon like such a good idea.

Rattinger put his arm around Brandon's shoulders and said, "Don't worry, kid. I won't hold it against you."

What a hoot this guy was, Brandon thought, as Rattinger strolled off laughing.

Movement caught the corner of Brandon's eye, and he thought he saw his sister, Brenda, among the sun worshipers—same long dark hair, same body shape. But he knew even before he saw the girl's face that it couldn't be her. Brenda and a bunch of her friends had actually chosen to go to summer school for a little enrichment. Of course, the class they had chosen to take was only drama, hardly a difficult academic subject, but it meant that she was firmly booked every weekday morning for the next few weeks.

At dinner, Brenda could speak of nothing but "the method," and "projection," and "sense memory," and how cute her teacher, Mr. Chris Suiter, was.

But a morning class did not explain why she never showed up at the beach in the afternoon. Even if the Walshes weren't members of the club, she could have gotten in because she was Brandon's sister or as the guest of one of her friends. The answer had to be that she didn't want to get in. And Brandon knew why.

At the club she was likely to run into Dylan.

Brenda and her boyfriend, Dylan McKay, had broken up while the previous semester was still in progress. Though she liked Dylan, maybe even loved him, she felt that she couldn't handle the speed with which their relationship was moving. The breakup made neither Brenda nor Dylan happy, but she was determined to have nothing to do with him till she was satisfied that she'd gotten a grip on her life.

Brandon thought Brenda's machinations were a little loony, but he'd never been in love. What did he know?

The wind picked up and shadows lengthened, and though the sun would take another few hours to set, people began to leave the club. Surfers tromped out of the water like prehistoric creatures climbing onto land for the first time. One of them broke from the crowd and walked toward the table where Brandon was folding towels.

It was Dylan, Brenda's erstwhile boyfriend and a good friend of Brandon's. Dylan was a very private guy, but Brandon had gotten closer to him than most people, and Dylan had opened up a little. This was a tough time for Dylan anyway because the police, the FBI, and maybe the Untouchables were looking for his father. Evidently Mr. McKay was heavy into white-collar crime: a little question of stocks, bonds, and securities, that kind of stuff.

A lot of people, like Mr. Walsh, suspected that Dylan was just as big a crook as his father, but anybody who really knew Dylan knew better. Brandon trusted him and so did Brenda. Even Mrs. Walsh seemed willing to give him the benefit of the doubt. They all could be wrong, but Brandon liked to trust his gut feelings.

Brandon set down a half-folded towel and called, "Yo, Dylan! How you doing?"

They shook hands. Dylan's were clammy from the cold water. Dylan said, "Getting by. Henry still lets me park my board here even though Pop stopped being a member."

Henry was in charge of support services at the Beverly Hills Beach Club. He was also Brandon's boss and a monster soap-opera fan. Woe be unto he who interrupted Henry during "The Young and the Restless." Brandon agreed that Henry was cool; then he glanced across the tanning deck and said, "Sandy's cool, too."

"Sandy is exquisite. But don't tell her I said so."

They spent some happy time admiring Sandy as she worked. She was a compact blonde who was a few years older than Brandon. She might even have been out of college, if she'd ever been in college. At the moment, she was serving a tall drink with a paper umbrella in it to an old woman who looked astonishingly like George Washington. Brandon agreed that Sandy really knew how to fill out her beach club uniform.

After a moment, Brandon said, "Sorry about you and Brenda."

Dylan shrugged. "It's just one of those things."

"Yeah, well, as far as I'm concerned, you can visit me at home any time you want."

They wished each other well. Dylan walked toward the locker room and Brandon hefted his pile of folded towels. You never knew who would want a towel. You'd need Carl Sagan to count them all. Billions and billions of towels.

While he distributed them, Brandon sometimes caught a look at Steve as he played volleyball with his California goddess. He let her make points. He let her give him clues on the fine art of serving. He let her spike the ball into his face. From the sand, he smiled like a goof and gave Brandon the thumbs-up sign. Steve wasn't very subtle, but you had to give him credit for tenacity.

When the towels were about gone, Henry called Brandon over and said, "I know this is going to break your heart, Walsh, but I want you to help Sandy set up the buffet table for the new members' mixer."

Brandon nodded and said, "It's a dirty job, but somebody—you know."

"I know."

Brandon found Sandy out by the patio arranging forks in an artistic spiral on a damask-covered table the length of a bowling alley. She suggested that Brandon fold napkins. Why not? Napkins would be a nice change.

From where they were, they had a pretty good view of the volleyball courts. Steve was on the sand again, and shortly allowed the California girl to help him to his feet.

Sandy said, "It's amazing how low a rich kid will sink to impress a major babe."

"Rich kids have no corner on *that* particular market."

"Maybe not. But I'll tell you something, Brandon: I've been working at this club for two seasons and I discovered one thing. The rich are different from you and me."

Brandon had heard that sentiment before. Now, where—? Oh, yeah. He smiled and said, "That's from *The Great Gatsby* by F. Scott Fitzgerald. As I recall, Hemingway's reply was, 'Yeah, the difference is that the rich have more money.'"

"Very good," said Sandy. "Glad to see there are still some readers out there." She got very involved with her silverware. Without looking at Brandon, she said, "When I read *Gatsby* you probably weren't even born yet."

"I don't know. That depends on how old you want me to be."

Sandy didn't have a good answer to that so she changed the subject. They had a long discussion about what was hot and what was not, whether being a vegetarian was worth the grief, if surfers were crazy. Neither of them talked about what was really on their minds, what was really on Brandon's mind, anyway. Was Sandy too old? Was Brandon too young? Did age matter if people liked each other? Was this all getting a little too serious?

The sun went down, preparations for the mixer were completed, and prospective club members began to arrive. Brandon saw a couple of tuxedos in the crowd—worn by guys who were *really* insecure, Brandon guessed—but most men wore Hawaiian shirts and sport coats or variations, and most women seemed comfortable in light sleeveless summer dresses. His parents had not yet arrived, which was a surprise. They were generally nauseatingly punctual; if an invitation asked them to be at a place at seven, they arrived no later than seven oh five. Still, who knew how hideous the traffic was on Pacific Coast Highway?

A live band began to play hits of the '60s and Brandon could not help bopping a little as he got people drinks and handed around hors d'oeuvres. When he retired behind the buffet table, Sandy grabbed him and forced him to dance to "I Can't Get No Satisfaction." Brandon protested that he was no dancer, but she held on tight and he managed to shuffle around without injuring either of them.

Henry came by, and while grinning reminded them that it was against beach club rules for employees to be seen having a good time in public.

"Brandon!" Mrs. Walsh called.

Brandon saw his mom and dad crossing the dance floor.

Henry winked at Brandon and Sandy, and said, "See you later." He hustled off to check on his other people.

"Hey, guys," Brandon said. "Good to see you. Where's Brenda?"

"Talking to Grandma on the phone," Mrs. Walsh said.

"Huh?" asked Brandon.

"That's what *I* said," Mrs. Walsh said. "But maybe it's true. They were still talking when we left."

Brandon knew that even if Brenda was still on the phone, that wasn't why she wasn't at the club.

Mr. and Mrs. Rattinger joined the group. Mrs. Rattinger was a little older than Brandon's mom, and she was nice-looking for a woman her age. She had a really terrific tan, but she smelled of cigarette smoke even when she wasn't smoking. Rattinger got a lot of mileage out of how late the Walshes were. "Rumor has it you took a wrong turn at Topanga." Brandon enjoyed Mr. Rattinger's sharp line of patter, but he could see that Dad was having a little trouble controlling his impatience with the gag.

"Well," said Rattinger, "we'll forgive you for being late as long as you pay your dues on time. Then your son can lay around on the beach like a lox with the other kids."

"Works for me," said Brandon and grinned.

"Don't get any ideas," Mr. Walsh said sourly.

What was *wrong* with the guy? He could be such a grump.

Mrs. Walsh said, "Jim, we really should find a table before they're all taken."

Mr. Walsh nodded and allowed his wife to lead him away.

To Brandon, Rattinger said, "Thanks again for the call today."

"No big deal. I call 'em as I see 'em."

"Yeah, well, we have to get you out on a paddle tennis court yourself, teach you a few tricks."

"Any time."

While he watched Mr. Rattinger show-boat through the crowd with his wife, glad-handing other members as if he were a politician,

Brandon said, "It really is a small world. My dad's an executive tax specialist, and he just started working on the Rattinger account."

When Sandy said nothing, Brandon looked at her. She turned away from him and began to fill wineglasses with chablis. "Small world," she agreed. But she wasn't happy about it.

There was a run on the buffet so it was a long time before Brandon had a chance to find out what was bothering Sandy. And then Henry took him away to help clean up. Brandon was stuffing used paper plates into plastic trash bags when Steve came up to him and said, "Here you are, Walsh. I've been looking all over for you."

"Right here, bro. Hauling trash is a nice change from folding towels." He hefted a trash bag into a dumpster. It thumped as the bag hit bottom.

"Whatever. The important thing is that it's party time: the grunion are running."

"It's a little late for a race, but I hope your grunion wins."

"Walsh, you slay me. Grunion are fish, and they run when they want to."

"Like I said, I hope your grunion—"

"Don't be obtuse, Walsh. What grunion do is just *called* running. They are the ultimate party fish. A couple of nights every summer they come to the beach to, as it were, lay their eggs.

It's a very happening scene. The usual gang will be there. You can bring your, uh, new friend if you like." Steve leaned toward Brandon and did a Groucho with his eyebrows.

Brandon tied up another trash bag and readied himself to lift it. Amazing how heavy paper could be. He said, "I'm sure Sandy has better things to do than hang with a bunch of high school kids."

"Maybe. But my guess is that she wouldn't mind hanging with one high school kid in particular."

"Steve—"

"Keep your shirt on. It's just an opinion."

Who was Brandon kidding? Did it really bother him at some level he wasn't even aware of that Sandy was an older woman? Who knew? Brandon suspected he did not have enough levels to make a question like that meaningful. And if he wanted to invite a friend to see party fish party, so what? It was late. He'd been running himself ragged for almost fifteen hours. He wasn't thinking very clearly.

By the time he got back to the buffet table, most of the guests were gone and somebody was sweeping up cigarette butts and dirty napkins. Sandy was taking apart the champagne fountain. She looked as tired as Brandon felt.

Brandon forged ahead. What could he lose? He came up next to her and began putting unused glasses into compartments in a cardboard box. He said, "Listen, I know this is kind of last minute, and it's cool to say no, but if you're not doing anything tonight, the grunion are running."

She loaded the pieces of the fountain onto an aluminum cart. "Really? I prefer the submarine races myself."

"Submarine races?"

"You really are from out of town, aren't you?" She pushed the cart away.

Brandon ran after her. "Yeah, Minneapolis. What do you say?"

Sandy stopped, but did not look at Brandon. He could see her clutching the cart's handle. She said, "Grunion can come ashore anywhere between Point Conception and the Mexican border. And after living in Los Angeles for twelve years, I have never seen so much as a grunion fin let alone a complete grunion. Lots of luck."

She started to push away, but Brandon grabbed the cart and said, "Did I say something wrong?"

Sandy sighed, and asked, "Why didn't you introduce me to your parents?"

"I'm sorry. I didn't know you cared about stuff like that."

"Don't flatter yourself." She shook the cart free of Brandon's grasp, and walked away. Still mystified, all Brandon could do was follow.

2

A money thing

BRANDON WENT AROUND THE CART AND
stood in Sandy's way. She stopped and steamed,
but did not try to get by. Brandon said, "Come
on, Sandy. I'm sorry. I really am."

Sandy shook her head and seemed to deflate
a little. She said, "It's not you, Brandon. It's just
that even though your parents seem like very nice
down-to-earth types, I'm not really taken with the
whole Beverly Hills whoopee."

"I told you. We're from Minnesota."

"But you go to West Beverly Hills High
School."

"Is the problem that I live in Beverly Hills

or that I go to high school?"

Sandy shook her head and lifted her hand as if to ward off Brandon's questions. "It's been a long day, Brandon, especially for an old broad like me. I can't tell one problem from another."

Brandon made a sweeping gesture and said, "Then come with me to a place where there are no problems, where ten thousand wild and crazy grunion are having an orgy on the beach." He waited, hoping he hadn't blown the whole game with his lighthearted approach.

Sandy said, "Let me think about it."

Better than no. But Brandon felt obligated to go on. He said, "I better warn you that some of my friends from high school will be down there, if that makes a difference to you."

"Does it make a difference to *you*?"

"No."

Sandy smiled and said, "Then let's go find us some party fish." She grabbed his hand and Brandon felt excitement that seemed to zap away his fatigue. They finished cleaning up and went down to the beach.

Brandon was pleased to see that Sandy had no problem fitting in with his friends, and they accepted her without question. He and Dylan had both been right. Sandy was very cool, and not exactly decrepit.

They waited on the beach for hours, but the grunion never arrived. The ocean was beautiful at night, and that held them for a while. The foam glowed like ghosts as the waves curled and rolled in, crashing against the beach with their ancient rhythm. The sea air whipped around them as they huddled together for warmth as much as for companionship. Sitting tight against Sandy felt good, but just sitting soon lost its charm and Brandon was not much for public necking. He wondered when the last bus left for Beverly Hills. Could he catch a ride with somebody?

Steve kept asking them to wait just ten minutes more, just five minutes. People at the edge of the crowd snuck away, and after another half hour or so, the only ones left were Sandy, Brandon, and Steve. Sandy said she had to work the next day, gave Brandon a peck on the cheek, and staggered up the beach.

"Sorry, man," Brandon said to Steve, not feeling a bit sorry, "but I can't let her walk to her car alone."

Steve grumbled something under his breath and leaped to his feet. He and Brandon walked Sandy to her car. The night was black except where scattered lamps lit bright islands. Brandon got another peck, and Sandy drove away. He and Steve stood there for a while with their hands in their pockets, contemplating the night and the ocean.

"Cold, man," Brandon said.

Steve made a nod that was half a shiver. "Need a ride?"

Steve drove him home, and Brandon barely got his clothes off before he collapsed into bed.

The next morning, Brenda caught him in the kitchen trying to pry his eyes open with a cup of coffee. She complained about the mess he'd left in the bathroom, but it was just to let him know she still existed. She wasn't really angry.

"What are you doing with Mom's winter coat?" Brandon asked. She was hugging it, petting it, occasionally sniffing it.

"It's for school."

That made no sense at all to Brandon. He was about to ask her for more of an explanation when Mr. Walsh entered looking at the morning paper. Everybody wished everybody else a good morning. Mr. Walsh left the paper on the breakfast bar, and got himself a cup of coffee and a bowl of fruit chunks.

"So, Dad," Brandon said, "you and Mom left on the early side last night."

Mr. Walsh looked up, surprised. "Did we? I guess we did." His eye caught something in the paper.

Brenda poured a bowl of whole-grain cereal, lifted the cover of the sugar bowl, thought better of it, and lowered the cover. She poured milk over her cereal and said, "I hear it's definitely going to be a Beverly Hills Beach Club kind of summer."

Mr. Walsh shrugged and looked at Mrs. Walsh as she came in with a fistful of birds-of-paradise. Mr. Walsh got very involved in complimenting their beauty and comparing them to the beauty of his wife.

Brandon and Brenda looked at each other with speculation. Brenda said, "It *will* be a beach club kind of summer, won't it?"

Mr. Walsh said, "No, it won't."

Brandon felt as if he'd somehow been betrayed. It was like his parents didn't approve of the place he worked, of the friends he was making. He said, "I don't get it. You had a good time at the party last night, didn't you?"

"Absolutely," Mrs. Walsh said.

"And you both love the beach."

"Absolutely," Mrs. Walsh said again.

"Then it must be a money thing," Brandon said. Sometimes he thought his parents would have them living in a cardboard box if they thought they could get away with it.

"It's not *just* a money thing," Mr. Walsh said uneasily.

"Then what thing is it, Dad?" Brandon's tone was very sarcastic.

Mr. Walsh answered with his intense and serious Dad voice that he used for handing down commandments carved on stone tablets.

He said, "Hobnobbing with the Jerry Rattingers of the world can be a lot of fun for a night, or maybe even two, but in the long run, it's much safer to keep your professional life and your social life separate."

"What social life?" Brenda asked. When she saw her mother's disapproving stare, Brenda said, "Sorry. I couldn't help myself."

Brandon was getting angry. With a wave of their hands, his parents were ruining his life. Everybody he knew was a member of the beach club. *Jerry Rattinger* was a member of the beach club. What would they think if his parents refused to join? Maybe Dad was cutting their financial throats, too, and they would end up living in that cardboard box after all. "Is the club way too Beverly Hills chi-chi for your Minnesota tastebuds?"

Mr. Walsh looked to his wife for support. "Did I say anything like that?"

She shook her head.

Brandon said, "You've definitely decided not to join."

"I'm sorry, Brandon," Mr. Walsh said.

"And there's nothing either of us can say or do to change your mind."

"What else is there to say, Brandon?"

"That's exactly my point, Dad." Brandon had to get moving. He was too frustrated to sit still, and arguing with his parents always proved to be unpleasant. He stood up and said, "Thanks for breakfast, Mom."

"Where are you going?" Mr. Walsh asked angrily.

Brandon considered saying, *an opium den*, but decided against it. "To the beach club."

"I thought today was your day off," Mrs. Walsh said.

"It is." Brandon went up to his room, got his gear and left, closing the front door as quietly as he could. Slamming a door was so tacky. Besides, if he left quietly, they would have to hunt for him or wonder if he was still there.

Brenda loved her drama class and she loved the drama teacher, Mr. Suiter, but at the moment Mr. Suiter was making Andrea cry. Andrea Zuckerman was the editor of the school paper, the *Beverly Blaze*. She was a person who did not normally show emotion, so Mr. Suiter had a difficult time getting her started. But once she began, Andrea's breath came in great sobs and the tears were never-ending.

Andrea was sitting on a chair atop a small riser in the middle of the big green room. Brenda, the other kids, and Mr. Suiter watched her with great intensity, but nobody moved to comfort her. Brenda knew this was just a sense-memory exercise, but she could not help feeling edgy about Andrea's discomfort. For a moment, she thought Andrea was really upset about something. Andrea tried to blink away her tears but they just kept coming. She buried her face in her hands.

"Thank you, Andrea," said Mr. Suiter. "That was terrific."

Like the others, Brenda applauded enthusiastically. Andrea looked up and smiled through her tears while she rubbed the corners of her eyes with the heels of her hands.

Mr. Suiter whirled on the class and pointed at Andrea as he said, "Did you see the difference? Before, she was just acting upset. Now, she's an absolute mess."

Andrea and everyone else laughed. While she dabbed at her face with a tissue, Mr. Suiter said, "And now for something completely different: My next victim is Brenda."

Andrea went to sit with the group while Brenda took her place. She hugged her mother's heavy winter coat. This was great. This was real acting. And she absolutely loved it when Mr. Suiter talked about her in front of the class.

Mr. Suiter said, "I asked Brenda to bring in her mother's winter coat so we could demonstrate another sense-memory process." He turned to Brenda and asked her to tell the story about the coat.

It was a little embarrassing to share a

moment from her childhood with the class; some of the kids were complete strangers. But that's what acting was all about, wasn't it? Letting other people see your vulnerable side? She clutched the coat as she spoke.

Brenda had been five years old. She'd gone shopping with Brandon and her parents during winter, and had been told to stay with Brandon. But the escalator was really intriguing, and she went for a ride—up and down, up and down. When she got tired of riding, she didn't know where Brandon and her parents had gone. Brenda was absolutely panic-stricken. She would die of starvation right there in the department store, or she would freeze when they threw her out. All she had to look forward to was a long lonely death. But she kept moving and eventually found Brandon and her parents. Her mom caught her up in a big bear hug. "The feel and smell of Mom's wool coat is definitely something I'll never forget as long as I live."

"Wow," said David Silver. He was smart and funny, but kind of a geek. Brenda didn't understand why he was in the class with them.

"Wow is right," Mr. Suiter said. "But the sixty-four-thousand-dollar question is this: Can Brenda Walsh re-create the emotions of being lost and found by using the coat to help her remember the smell and texture of wet winter wool? I think she can."

The bell rang ending the period.

"We'll find out tomorrow whether I'm right."

Could Brenda do it? She'd have to really get in touch with the child that still existed within her. Clutching the coat, Brenda strolled from the room with Andrea and Donna. Donna asked if she could carry the coat and Brenda let her.

Donna almost dropped it. "It's the heaviest piece of clothing I ever held." She clutched it and sniffed it as Brenda had done.

Andrea said, "The tears came, but it was so forced. Something about it didn't feel right."

"Don't be so hard on yourself," Brenda said. "You did great. I thought you were really unhappy."

"You did?"

Donna said, "It must get really *really* cold back in Minnesota."

Brenda said, "Cold doesn't begin to describe it. For half the year you feel as if you're living inside an Eskimo Pie."

Kelly Taylor was waiting for them outside the door; she was dressed for the summer in cut-off jeans, sandals, and rad retro tie-dyed T-shirt. She was ready for anything, beach-wise. She said, "I get frostbite just thinking about winter in Minnesota. Who's for the beach?"

Kelly was this really hot blonde who had taught Brenda how to survive in the Bev Hills social scene, and they had become good friends,

maybe even best friends. Part of their friend-
ship rested on the fact that Brenda was a little
jealous of Kelly's cool mom and her never-ending
credit cards; and that Kelly was a little jealous of
Brenda's traditional home life.

"I'm there," Donna said.

Brenda caught herself frowning. You're an
actress, she told herself. You can carry off this
simple little scene. She said, "Have a good
time."

"You're not coming?" Kelly seemed genuinely surprised.

"I have this sense-memory exercise to do."
She took her coat back from Donna and stroked
it as if it were a cat.

"Give me a break," Kelly said.

"No, it's true, Kelly." David looked over the
top of their group. Brenda hadn't even noticed
him following them. David said, "A creative person must follow his *or her* creative impulses.
What Joseph Campbell calls his *or her* bliss."

"That's very well put, David," Brenda said.
He's still a geek, she thought.

David worked his way into the group
between Kelly and Donna, and said, "And since
Brenda will be following her bliss this afternoon, you now have room in your car to take
me to the beach instead."

Donna and Kelly looked at him as if he had
bad breath.

"Don't worry," he said. "I don't mind sitting in the back seat."

"Thanks," Kelly said to Brenda sarcastically.

When Kelly, Donna, and David were gone, Brenda asked Andrea what she had on the schedule.

They walked down the hall that led to the bus stop. Neither of them had a car. Andrea said, "Same thing you have: avoiding the beach."

"It's that obvious, huh?"

"Snow in July."

"If I ran into Dylan right now, I would just die. You know what I mean?"

Andrea nodded glumly and asked, "Does Brandon ever ask about me?"

Brenda put her hand on Andrea's shoulder, and was about to say something, but she didn't know what. Brandon was thoroughly involved with some older woman named Sandy.

Andrea said, "That's okay." She smiled, but it was less convincing than her tears had been earlier.

Brandon thought that playing paddle tennis with an old guy like Jerry Rattinger would be a cinch, but about three seconds into the game, he discovered he was wrong. Rattinger was a quick powerful guy, and one of the most motivated people Brandon had ever met.

Every time Brandon made a point, Brandon called, "Beginner's luck!" It was the truth and Rattinger bought it at first, but he became more skeptical about Brandon's luck with time. Brandon won at last, but only after losing gallons of sweat, and the score was very close. He somewhat mollified Rattinger by complimenting him on his teaching.

They showered and changed and met again at a table that was ringside to the volleyball courts and the tanning deck. The scenery—read girls—was positively incredible. Brandon and Rattinger made selections from the lunch menu, and then as they talked, their eyes wandered.

"So," said Rattinger, "what do you and your father talk about?"

"Not much, lately. We're both working so hard, we don't run into each other very often."

"That's just wrong," Rattinger said and scowled as if he were really angry. "You're a high school kid. If you can't have a real summer vacation now, when will you have it? Not when you have a wife and kids to support."

Brandon shook his head and said, "Tell it to my dad. He didn't want me to go out for hockey because it conflicted with my paper route."

They were silent while they watched a couple of bodacious bodies undulate across the patio to the tanning deck. This was incredible, not only the girls, but the fact that he and Jerry Rattinger were having lunch together and he was talking to Brandon as if they were equals. Incredible!

Rattinger said, "Far be it from me to criticize your father. He seems like a very sincere man, and a very hard-working guy, but he doesn't understand that life is different out here from what it was back in the corn belt. Making it in L.A. is all about perception. It's not what you are but what other people think you are. Get me?"

"Gotcha." What Rattinger said made sense. Dad was shooting himself in the foot by not joining the beach club. Brandon watched as Sandy walked onto the other side of the patio and put out four setups on each table.

Rattinger leaned toward him and asked secretively, "So, what kind of wheels are you lusting after?"

"A sixty-five Mustang convertible."

"I had one of those." A girl in a yellow spandex outfit walked by, keeping time with her hips. Rattinger said, "I had one of those, too." He shook his head and smiled. "But that was a long time ago in a galaxy far, far away. Now I'm a happily married guy with a wife, two girls, two cats, and a dog." He noticed Sandy and called to her impatiently, "Sandy, can someone take our order, or are we invisible?"

"I'll send Jeannie right over."

Sandy passed them. When she was gone, Rattinger said, "Talk about a piece of work."

Brandon could only agree.

After lunch, Rattinger had business elsewhere, but Brandon hung around to see his friends. Steve caught him at the table and confided that the grunion would be running again that evening.

"What do you mean, again?" Brandon asked.

"Trust me," said Steve. "Grunion gotta run and birds gotta fly."

"I trust you, Steve. I just don't trust the grunion."

Brandon slapped Steve on the back and went to make a special arrangement. It had worked for Butch and Sundance. Maybe it would work for him.

After the arrangement was made, he looked around and eventually found Sandy in the office signing out her receipts. She was about to leave for home, and Brandon offered to drive her.

"In what?" she asked. It was common knowledge that Brandon didn't have a car.

"Come on. I'll show you."

Brandon had rented a tandem bicycle. At first Sandy was reluctant to ride with him— "We'll break our silly necks," were her exact words—but Brandon egged her on and at last they were off.

Brandon found that riding tandem was more difficult than riding alone, especially with a partner who was as inexperienced as he was. They spent a lot of time overcorrecting for each other's attempts to balance, but as far as Brandon was concerned, the danger and frantic screams were part of the fun.

They rode to the end of a cement walkway, locked up the bike, and carefully picked their way out onto a pile of rocks that tumbled into the ocean. The rocks were slick with algae and sharp with barnacles. The air had never smelled so fresh. Here, with this woman, Brandon felt more alive than he had all summer.

They sat for a long time, watching the sun grow more orange as it set, smelling the smells, feeling the wind. A flock of pelicans effortlessly flew by in formation.

Brandon said, "Some day I'm going to be a zillionaire and live near the beach."

"Oh, really?" Sandy appraised him with disbelief.

"Yes, I'm going to start a conglomerate called Cabana Boys R Us. I'll be chairman of the board, and you can be executive director of everything else."

"Just what I always wanted to be: Grand High Poobah."

A long silence followed, during which the sun touched the horizon and the wind developed a cold edge. Brandon thought about what being a zillionaire might be like. He didn't know what Sandy was thinking about; she seemed to be concentrating on a point far out at sea. She shook her head.

"What?" Brandon asked.

"I don't know. It just . . . Listening to you makes me realize that I'm never going to have a beach house or most of the other things I used to dream about when I was your age."

"You're not dead yet."

"No. But I'm getting older by the minute." She shivered, and said, "We better get back," but didn't actually move.

Brandon didn't want their afternoon to end like this, with Sandy feeling like some kind of refugee from an old folks home. He said, "So, you don't want to wait for the grunion?"

Sandy smiled wistfully and touched Brandon's cheek. "You're very sweet. You know that, don't you?"

That sounded like a cue to Brandon. He leaned toward her a little and said, "And you're very pretty." His words were almost lost in the crashing of the waves.

"Damn it, kid, how old *are* you?"

They both smiled as they connected. If this was old age, Brandon would take a dozen.

Brandon had never been kissed with such expertise, with such passion. His entire being was recharged.

They rode the tandem back to the beach club and made a movie date for the next evening. As he bussed home, Brandon really felt fine.

The next day when he got off work, Brandon searched for Sandy. He passed Steve, who was putting the moves on a dark-haired girl named Maia. She was very pretty, but in Brandon's opinion, a little too young for Steve. Brandon smiled. He was hardly in a position to make judgments about age.

When Brandon found Sandy, he saw that she'd obviously been crying. She apologized for breaking their date and ran off, leaving Brandon feeling very much at a loss. He wanted to comfort her, but was frustrated by the fact that he didn't know what her problem was.

And then Jerry Rattinger found Brandon and made him a proposition that stunned him. When Brandon went home and reported the proposition to his parents, they were also stunned, and not nearly so delighted.

Mr. Walsh asked, "Rattinger wants to buy you a car?"

"He's not buying me anything. He's just giving me an advance on my salary."

That seemed pretty straightforward to

Brandon, but Dad insisted on taking the deal apart, strand by strand.

Mr. Walsh asked, "Salary for what?"

"Well, this summer I'll probably be more like a gofer, but once school starts, he says I can work as a trainee in his publicity office, kind of tie it in with the school paper." The school angle was always good.

While Mr. Walsh considered that, Mrs. Walsh asked, "What about the beach club?"

"Henry's got to understand. Rattinger's paying me double my salary no matter how many hours I work, even on days he doesn't need me. It's a win-win situation."

"I still don't understand, Brandon," Mr. Walsh said. "Why is he paying you to do nothing? Just because he likes the cut of your jib?"

Brandon shrugged and said, "You know what he's like, Dad. His philosophy of life is different from yours. And I think he feels sorry for me because he knows a teenager in L.A. without a car has no life. And even though he has two beautiful little girls, I think that deep down inside he really wants a son."

Mr. Walsh seemed to be in shock. He wanted to speak, but he almost couldn't get the words out. "I think you're right, Brandon. I just didn't expect him to go after mine."

Could Dad really believe that? Did he really believe that Rattinger could purchase Brandon with an automobile? Evidently so. Brandon had never seen him so bummed. Before Brandon had a chance to explain, Mr. Walsh said he was going to bed, and walked quickly from the room.

Brandon had trouble sleeping that night. Not only because he had upset Dad so much, or even because Dad refused to understand the motives of either Brandon or Rattinger, but because the discussion had not been finished. Dad had walked off like a zombie before anything could be decided. Brandon had tried to go after him, but Mom said, "Let him cool down, Brandon. Talk to him tomorrow."

The next morning, while still lying in bed, Brandon thought of an entirely new take on the situation. He got up, dressed, and went next door to Brenda's room to test it out and gather a little support.

Brenda was standing in the middle of her room wearing shorts, a T-shirt, and Mom's heavy winter coat. She refused to tell him why she was wearing it in the middle of a hot California summer, but she agreed to listen to Brandon. She listened impatiently.

Brandon stood in Brenda's doorway gesticulating as he made his case. "Rattinger warned me that Dad might try to torpedo the deal, but I said, 'no way.' The car's not a gift, after all. And then this morning, it struck me. He really doesn't want me to have *any* car because he's still punishing me for totaling Mondale."

Brenda seemed preoccupied with the coat. She stroked it as she said, "I don't know, Brandon. Dad stood by you when you had to go to traffic court. And he knows you haven't had a drink since the accident."

"Then what's his problem, Brenda?"

Brenda stopped stroking and fixed Brandon with a steely eye. "I think that's *fairly* obvious."

"That business about buying sons with cars?"

"It's a real possibility. Why else would this man offer to pay you good money this summer for doing practically nothing? The truth is, I think Dad's right."

"You're as bad as he is."

"What can I say? We're related. And if it's really bothering you this much, you should talk to him. After all, it doesn't matter whether *I* agree with you."

Brenda was right. It was time for the shoot-out at the OK Breakfast Table.

3

A million stories

BUT WHEN BRANDON WENT DOWNSTAIRS, his mother told him that his father had gone to San Diego for an audit. Relief, anger, and frustration boiled through Brandon all at once.

Mrs. Walsh said, "He wanted me to tell you that whatever you decided about Mr. Rattinger would be fine with him, and that he'd talk to you about it when he gets home."

Brandon had really been ready to do this, and now his resolve was all dressed up with nowhere to go. He tried to maintain cool. With extreme patience, he said, "I have the late shift. By the time I get home, he'll be in bed."

Brandon shook his head and said, "This is so typical. After making me feel guilty about not wanting to work so hard this summer, he's working so hard himself that he has no time to talk to me."

Mrs. Walsh set a glass of orange juice in front of Brandon and said, "Can't it keep for one night?"

Well, couldn't it? Brandon said, "I guess it'll have to."

It would keep in the real world, but all the way to work, inside his head, Brandon ran through a dialogue with his father. He ran it over and over again. Sometimes Brandon won. Sometimes Mr. Walsh won. But the discussuion always entailed a lot of shouting and bad feelings all around. Not exactly a win-win situation.

At the beach club, Brandon found Rattinger playing paddle tennis. He waited till the game was over, and when Rattinger approached to greet him, Brandon explained the situation as it stood.

Rattinger said, "It sounded like a perfect fit. I needed an assistant. You needed a car. But if I'm getting between you and your dad, forget it."

Brandon didn't want to forget it. He didn't want to change fathers, but he did want a car. He saw no reason why he couldn't do one and still not do the other. He said, "Well, my dad did say that whatever I choose would be cool with him."

Still serious, Rattinger asked, "So, it's still a Mustang convertible, right?"

"Right." This could work. This could be very, very good.

Though he'd straightened things out with Rattinger, Brandon still felt rotten because he hadn't straightened things out with his father. While walking through the beach club, still grinding over what he ought to say, ought to do, he saw Steve demonstrating the finer points of volleyball to young Maia. Brandon found Sandy putting setups down on the patio tables. He was positive she'd seen him, but she continued to pretend he wasn't there.

"Hi," said Brandon brightly. "Are we feeling any better today?"

"I don't know how *you* are feeling today, Brandon, but *I* am feeling a lot worse. So consider yourself warned."

It can't be me, Brandon thought. We haven't spoken together since yesterday, and before that we were fine. Maybe he could help. He said, "Do you want to talk about it?"

Sandy stopped what she was doing, but continued glaring at the table. She said, "Look, Brandon, you're really a sweet boy, but I'm going through some very heavy personal stuff right now, and I'm not about to pour out my heart to a teenager from Beverly Hills."

Brandon could only gape at her as she put down her last fork, her last spoon, and walked away. Henry saw the whole interchange, but could not explain Sandy to Brandon except to say, "'There are a million stories in the Naked City,' Brandon. Well, that's nothing compared to what's going on at this beach club."

Which, as far as Brandon was concerned, was colorful but useless. He saw Sandy a few more times that day, but he didn't approach her, and she acted as if he didn't even exist. Brandon folded another million towels, delivered another million drinks, solved another million tiny crises. When his shift was over, the air was still warm and the sun would still be up for another hour or so. He sat on a low stucco wall and, for a change, just enjoyed being at the beach.

Steve came by and settled next to him. He was sunburned except for the spot on his nose where he had applied a greasy green sunblock. His hair was wild and he kept running his hands through it. He waved at his very young friend as she walked by with her mother. Evidently beauty ran in the family.

Steve said, "Her name is Maia Landen. She's young, but she's really cute, don't you think?"

"I know her name, Steve. You've only told me it four or five times since lunch. But exactly how young is she?"

Steve shrugged. "I don't know. Young. But she's very mature for her age."

"Steve," Brandon said disapprovingly.

"I haven't made my move yet. I'm just . . ."

Evidently, Steve couldn't decide just *what* because rather than fill in the blank, he changed the subject. "So, how about you and Sandy?"

"Our relationship is kind of like, you know, a grunion. Like, who knows if it really exists?"

"Sounds like me and Kelly."

While Steve and Brandon pondered the mysterious nature of relationships, Henry came by looking for a couple of strong backs to help Mr. Rattinger in the parking lot.

On the lot, Rattinger was standing next to a black BMW, bouncing a set of car keys in one hand. The car had recently been polished so that it shined like a panther, like a pool of ink. The chrome was bright enough to answer questions. Steve looked upon it with lust.

What a way to live, Brandon thought. He asked, "You need me to haul something upstairs for you, Mr. Rattinger?"

"No," said Rattinger seriously. "I need you to get behind the wheel of this vehicle to find out if it's something you wouldn't mind driving this summer."

Brandon was so astonished, he could think of nothing to say. The guy must really like the cut of his jib. Whatever that meant.

Rattinger said, "You said you needed a car."

With conscious effort, Brandon closed his mouth. Then he said, "I was thinking more about a used Mustang."

"We can still get you the 'stang if you want, but meanwhile, my corporation can lease the Beemer and deduct the interest."

Steve was leaning in at the window of the car, appreciating it as if it were a woman.

Brandon called, "Don't drool on the upholstery, Steve."

Steve said, "This is an outstanding piece of equipment."

Rattinger threw the keys to Brandon and said, "Why don't you take a little cruise up the coast, let me know how this hunk of junk handles."

The keys seemed solid enough, but Brandon still wasn't sure he was awake. "Mr. Rattinger, I don't know what to say."

"How about, 'Thanks, Jerry,'?"

Steve said, "If I say 'Thanks, Jerry' do I get a car, too?"

"Don't forget to buckle up," Rattinger said and took a few steps before he snapped his fingers and turned back to Brandon. "I hate to ask you to do this."

Brandon said, "That's okay." Sheesh, Brandon thought. The guy just gave me a BMW to play around with. What did he want? More towels? A paddle tennis partner? Whatever Rattinger wanted, Brandon was there.

"Excuse us for a moment," Rattinger said to Steve, and put his arm around Brandon's shoulders. As they walked away from the car, Rattinger said, "Apparently, Mrs. Rattinger had a bit too much sun with her white wine this afternoon, and she's going to need a lift home. I would take her myself, but I need to tie up a few loose ends down here."

Here he was hobnobbing with Jerry Rattinger. Now the guy was asking him to do personal favors. This had gone way beyond the relationship that would exist between an employer and the hired help. Jerry Rattinger was his friend. "No problem, Jerry," Brandon said.

He and Steve waited with the car while Rattinger went to get his wife. Steve leaned against the front fender, trying to be cool, but Brandon could tell that he was impressed by what had just happened. He said, "Brandon, do you know what kind of girls we could pick up with a heap like this?"

"What about Maia?"

"Maia is only the beginning," Steve said, and winked.

Rattinger escorted his wife onto the parking lot. She looked healthy enough to Brandon, but what did he know about women that age?

Rattinger gave her a peck on the cheek, which she endured with barely disguised annoyance, and held open the back door for her. Mrs. Rattinger got into the BMW without speaking to anyone and lit up a cigarette while she waited.

"Drive carefully, Brandon."

"No problem, Jer."

Rattinger and Steve watched as Brandon started the engine. It roared and then hummed. Brandon waved and set off. With this suspension system, the parking lot felt as if it were paved with glass.

As they drove up Pacific Coast Highway in the deepening darkness, Brandon tried to study the control panel. Outside the starship *Enterprise,* he'd never seen so many buttons, levers, and switches. He wanted to turn on the headlamps, but he'd have to wait till he hit a red light before he'd be able to find the right control. Maybe the lights went on by themselves. Who knew?

After a few miles, Brandon noticed Mrs. Rattinger studying him in the rearview mirror. She puffed furiously on her long, slim cigarette and asked, "So, when did you start working for my husband?"

"About fifteen minutes ago." Why did she sound so angry? Maybe she really *had* had too much sun.

"What do you think of him so far?"

"He's the greatest."

Mrs. Rattinger puffed some more and flicked her ash onto the floor. The ash hurt Brandon but he figured, well, it was really her husband's car. She said, "You don't have to put on an act for me, my friend. I just hope he's making this trip worth your while."

Worth his while? Money? Jerry was his friend. Besides, how do you say no to a guy who's lent you a dream car for the summer? Brandon said, "Mrs. Rattinger, I'm sorry but I don't know what you're talking about."

"I'm talking about my husband."

Brandon waited for more but it didn't come. He was still confused when he pulled into the left-turn lane at Sunset and waited for the green arrow. Was that the switch for the headlamps? Did Mrs. Rattinger have a point or was she just ranting?

She said, "Don't think you're the first pretty boy he's hired to drive me home from the beach club so he can be with his playthings. I heard he's trying to get back with Sandy. I can't see it myself, she's so vapid. Is it true?"

Brandon didn't know if it was true, but he was shocked that Mrs. Rattinger felt it necessary to ask the question. He made his left turn, and while he drove east on Sunset and his mind tried to get a grip on the situation, he waited with fearful anticipation for Mrs. Rattinger to tell him more.

4

Having been had

ONCE MRS. RATTINGER GOT STARTED, she rambled all the way home. It just happened that Brandon was in the car; he got the impression that she was really talking to herself, recounting her husband's many infidelities wistfully, without anger, as if they were covered by scabs she was used to picking at. Sandy was just the latest mistress in a series of stewardesses, waitresses, shop girls, movie extras, and sports hopefuls.

Brandon had been had, big time. At first, he sank into a deep blue funk while he considered how stupid he'd been to be taken in by Jerry

Rattinger's big talk and blustery outgoing manner. The guy was a first-class jerk, and Brandon was a first-class jerk for believing anything he said.

Rattinger's house was a mansion high in the hills behind an ivy-covered wall. The grounds seemed to extend for miles around the two-story brick building. Brandon dropped off Mrs. Rattinger, and having problems of her own, she didn't notice what a black mood he was in. Even before Mrs. Rattinger made it to the front door, Brandon drove around the long circular drive back out into the street.

He found himself speeding. He took deep breaths and commanded himself to slow down. No point getting killed over a guy like Jerry Rattinger. Or a woman like Sandy. She'd had Brandon, too. She'd perfectly played the part of the poor but honest working girl whose only problem with Brandon was his age. If she was seeing both him and Rattinger, no wonder she was nervous, forever in a sweat that one or the other of them would find out. Lord knew what her relationship with Rattinger involved. He was obviously a man of big appetites. And after being kissed by Sandy, Brandon knew she could feed them.

Brandon's anger grew. He might be a jerk for believing Rattinger and Sandy, but he was no wuss who would go on playing their little game. Good-bye, car. Good-bye, Sandy. Good-bye, job.

It was dark by the time Brandon returned to the beach club. He took some time inspecting the BMW under the parking lot lights to make sure the paint and body work were as perfect as when Rattinger had given the car to him. He didn't want anybody accusing him of carelessness, not at a time like this. It would only confuse the issue.

The car was in good shape. Brandon took a last longing look at it and went to wait in the shadows among the trees at the foot of the stairway up to Rattinger's cabana.

Though it was high summer, the air seemed cool to Brandon, not the warm embrace it had been the evening before, or even earlier that evening. His state of mind could have accounted for the goose bumps on his arms. He was certain he was in no physical danger, but confrontations always made him uncomfortable, even when they were necessary and unavoidable. Unavoidable, yes. And better tonight when his anger and contempt were new than tomorrow or the next day when he might rationalize them away.

Brandon heard sharp footsteps approaching and he looked up from rubbing a callous that had developed at the spot where a deck chair rested when he carried it. Sandy came around the corner wearing a short pink dress and high-heeled shoes that matched the dress. She'd taken some time with her hair. Usually, clips held it back from her face; now, it hung in ringlets about her ears. Makeup made her look older, like a woman who'd been around.

Brandon waited till she'd stepped onto the stairway before he moved into the light and said, "Since you're going up to his cabana, you can give him back his car keys."

She turned and backed into the handrail as if Brandon had attacked her. He threw the BMW keys at her feet. She glanced at them and then at Brandon. She was still beautiful. Brandon could not help liking her even now. Which only made the situation worse. Sadly, she said, "It's not what you think, Brandon. It's not some cheap, sordid affair."

"How do you know what I think, Sandy? You don't know me. And I don't know you."

"Right," Sandy said. She angrily scooped up the keys. "You don't know me. You don't know what I go through every morning to face the world. You have no right to judge me, Brandon, especially when Mommy and Daddy still pay the bills."

A very low blow, Brandon thought. He also was in no mood to pull punches. "And who pays *your* bills, Sandy? You better go. Your sugar daddy is waiting for you."

Venetian blinds gently knocked against an upstairs window, and Brandon and Sandy looked up. Rattinger was looking down at them, his face half hidden in shadow. Brandon threw Rattinger a mock salute and walked away. Behind him, Sandy began to sob.

Brandon stood at the edge of Pacific Coast Highway for a long time, waiting for the bus to come. Across the wide street was a cliff that was occasionally lit by the lights of passing cars. The darkness of the cliff was a blank stage on which Brandon played out his thoughts.

Both Rattinger and Mr. Walsh agreed that Brandon should make his own decision regarding the car, regarding Rattinger's job offer, regarding what could well be a turning point in Brandon's life. Each of them assumed that Brandon would make the right decision, though for each of them, the right decision was *something else*. Rattinger had made deciding a lot easier for Brandon.

Brandon had his pick of seats on the bus. The only people aboard were the driver and three passengers—two old Latino women who conversed gaily, and a black man lost in his own thoughts. Brandon took a seat far away from everybody else and stared glumly out the window. How many of those guys out there driving cars got them by stepping on somebody's face? Riding the bus could be lonely, inconvenient, and proletarian. But it was also noble.

Brandon got off the bus and walked home

through the clean, silent Beverly Hills streets. Once, a police car slowly passed him but did not stop. Brandon could not decide if he was pleased or not that he looked so innocent.

Inside the house, Brandon found his father on the couch nodding over the book his parents read only when waiting up for their children. He wore a white shirt and gray slacks; his tie was loosened but still around his neck. Perhaps Mr. Walsh had just gotten home himself.

"Dad," Brandon said, pleasantly surprised. They had to talk. "I'm glad you're here. A lot of funky stuff is happening at work, and—"

"I hope that what I have to say will put your mind at ease about all that. On the train between here and San Diego, I had a lot of time to think."

Brandon had had a lot of time to think, too. He didn't want his father to torture himself this way. "Dad, I—"

"Brandon, please. Let me get this off my chest and then you can talk." Mr. Walsh swallowed and shook his head before he continued, using the same sincere tone. "It's one thing for a father to try instilling a sense of positive values into his children, but it's quite another thing when a father disguises his own frustrations as experience and wisdom."

"I don't follow you," Brandon said. This was not the conversation he'd expected—neither the encouragement to make his own decision, nor a demand that he see things his father's way.

Mr. Walsh shrugged and seemed to have difficulty speaking. Brandon did not feel very comfortable, himself. What was going on? Mr. Walsh said, "The other morning, when you asked if the reason we didn't join the beach club was because of *the money thing,* I managed to change the subject. But the truth is that the money thing is important, and I've been struggling with it ever since I turned down the promotion that would have moved us back to Minnesota. Not that I regret staying here." Brandon imagined that in the carpet, Mr. Walsh saw all that his decision had meant to his family.

"Dad, this is—"

"I'm sorry, Brandon. I know I'm rambling. The bottom line is this: Before you waste another moment folding deck chairs, do yourself a favor. Forget about your old man's hang-ups and go to work for Rattinger. See how the other half lives."

"Dad, believe me, I've seen all I want to."

"I'm sure Rattinger has his flaws. Everyone does." Mr. Walsh sighed. It had been a long day for both of them. "But he's smart. He's dynamic. And most importantly, he's a team player. And in this town that counts for everything."

Brandon knew that wasn't true. And he knew that *his dad* knew it wasn't true. Having made a mistake in one direction, Dad was now going just as wrong in the other.

"I want to say just one more thing. My father said it to me on the morning I left for college. He told me not to sell myself short. He told me to just be my own man, and after that everything else would fall into place. It was good advice then and it's good advice now."

My own man, Brandon thought. I barely escaped with my integrity intact. Being true to yourself was not always easy. As he got ready for bed, Brandon wondered if perhaps the more difficult it was to keep your integrity, the more important doing it was.

The next morning when the alarm went off, Brandon considered staying in bed. Getting up might not be worth the trouble. Jerry Rattinger was a big wheel at the Beverly Hills Beach Club. If he was unhappy with Brandon, just how much pressure would he have to apply before Brandon was history?

However, as far as he knew, Brandon still had a job. He pried himself out of bed, got ready for work, and rode the bus to the beach, where another perfect day was just beginning. The only thing happening this early was the sea gulls wheeling above the breakers calling insults to each other.

Brandon was surprised to find Rattinger in the locker room at this hour putting on his paddle tennis shoes. Brandon stiffened, but he had work to do. He *belonged* here. At least for the moment. Rattinger's presence wouldn't scare him away. Brandon would just ignore the guy. Brandon began to change into his uniform.

Without looking up, Rattinger said sarcastically, "Well, if it isn't the king of the cabana boys? I wondered if you were going to show your face this morning."

"I still have a commitment to the beach club."

"Did your father tell you to say that, or did you think of it all by yourself?"

There it was, Brandon thought, the reason for me to make the final break. Thank goodness the guy was nasty. Rattinger's question confirmed Brandon's opinion that the guy was a total jerk. Brandon had made the right decision. His dad's right decision. And it was right for Brandon, too.

While Brandon changed as quickly as he could, Rattinger ran through his stretching routine. Brandon thought he might escape from the locker room without having to defend himself again, but as he walked toward the door, Rattinger said, "It got very ugly last night. Very embarrassing. Very unnecessary." With genuine disappointment he said, "I could have taught you so much."

"Believe it or not, Mr. Rattinger, you've already taught me plenty." He had his hand on the doorknob when Brandon turned and said, "Thanks to you, Sandy's a nervous wreck."

"Sandy's an adult. As far as she is concerned, my conscience is clear. As far as you're concerned, I think Henry wants to see you." While the door swung closed behind Brandon, Rattinger called, "Good luck on your next job, kid."

Brandon couldn't help reflecting that he would probably be happier at his next job, whatever it was. A guy with folding experience could go anywhere. Maybe Nat would take him back at the Peach Pit. Brandon marched up to the office, and found Henry sucking on a protein shake and watching "The Young and the Restless."

Sounding more impatient than he wanted to, Brandon said, "Mr. Rattinger said you want to see me."

Henry picked up a remote control and froze his soap opera. He took another sip of his shake. He was taking forever. Brandon was going crazy. "Damn it, Henry, am I fired?"

Henry took his time appraising Brandon, and then said, "Rattinger ordered me to fire you. I told him I'd consider it."

"And?"

"I considered it and I rejected it. I don't want anybody around here getting the idea that everything is bought and paid for."

"That's great, Henry. Thanks. What about Sandy?"

"Sandy quit." Henry sounded sad.

"I thought she might."

"Yeah. But her troubles ain't nothing compared to what Julia has on 'The Young and the Restless.'"

Henry kept him for fifteen minutes explaining the ramifications of the current 'The Young and the Restless' plot. Brandon got lost, but continued to nod because Henry was having such a good time.

When Brandon broke free at last, he folded a stack of towels and took them down to the tanning deck. As he passed the paddle tennis courts, he heard Rattinger and Edgar having their usual argument about whether the ball had landed fair or not.

Edgar saw him and called, "You see it, Brandon?"

"Yes, sir." Brandon also saw the doomed look on Rattinger's face. Brandon knew what Rattinger would do if he were in Brandon's shoes, and Rattinger knew he knew.

"Wait a second," Rattinger said. "Why don't we just take it over?"

"What for?" asked Edgar. "The kid saw it. Brandon, what's the call?"

Brandon knew what Rattinger would do, but he was no longer playing by Rattinger's rules. He said, "It was in, Jerry."

Rattinger looked surprised. He and Brandon

both knew that in some important moral way, Brandon had scored a big one against the old Ratt-meister.

Brandon felt good, as if he'd won some kind of battle with evil. The feeling lasted while he delivered the rest of his towels. He passed the parking lot on his way back to the laundry and saw Sandy loading a beach bag full of stuff into the trunk of her car, a boxy old Japaneser no more fashionable than Mondale had been.

Brandon said, "You moving out?"

Sandy turned suddenly. Brandon was afraid she might be angry at him, but whatever fire had been in her was gone. She looked merely tired. She said, "I'm leaving town. My mom and my sister have a place up in Bakersfield." When she sniffled and her eyes began to well up, she turned back to the trunk and made a big production of arranging things as she spoke. "He told me he loved me, Brandon. He told me he'd leave his wife and kids. That was two years ago."

Brandon put his hand on her shoulder and slowly turned her around. He said, "I'm sorry."

Sandy shook her head and tried to smile. "Being with you, listening to you talk, made me see how jaded and angry I'd become. Thanks."

She kissed him, a single sisterly touch, and got into her car. Feeling a little weepy himself, Brandon watched her drive away.

■ ■ ■

Brenda sat in drama class smiling because she knew something nobody else knew, something she had not known herself until her father had told her *his* memory of that awful day she'd gotten lost at Dayton's Department Store.

She'd been running around the living room trying to capture that moment. She'd been sweating because she was wearing her mother's heavy coat, and crying, "Mommy! Mommy!" None of it worked. She was just a teenager sweating and acting like an idiot.

"Brenda?"

For a moment, Brenda felt relief that she'd been found by her father. Then she'd been embarrassed to remember that she wasn't really and that she wasn't really lost.

"Hi, Dad."

"Still trying to get in touch with your emotions?"

"Yes, but it's not working." Tears, real tears of frustration, had come. "And now I'm crying out of control."

"That was some scary day," Mr. Walsh had said. He shook his head.

"I know all about it," Brenda had said. She told the story to her dad just as she had told it to herself a thousand times. "Mom was in the linen department, and you'd gone upstairs to buy a new bowling ball. I was supposed to stay with Brandon, but I started riding the escalators, and that's when I got into trouble."

It was then that Mr. Walsh had given Brenda the clue she needed to accurately reproduce the emotions of the little girl Brenda had been.

Mr. Suiter called on her and she took the hot seat on the riser in the middle of the room. To the obvious delight of the other kids in class, Brenda explained what had happened that morning. "And then," Brenda said, "he told me that before I got lost, while I was still playing on the escalators, I was having the time of my life, and that I was cute."

"No lie, Brenda," Mr. Suiter said. "But so what?"

"So, all I'd been remembering was the part *after* I got lost. The part where I was hysterical. But when my dad told me how cute I'd been, something clicked inside." She tapped the side of her head. "I had been trying to feel something I'd never felt. Now, I realized it's not about the coat. It's about *me*! Being back on that escalator having a great time, just being all by myself."

"Breakthrough alert," Mr. Suiter cried. "We have a breakthrough at center stage."

Mr. Suiter was right, and she felt good to let it all come pouring out. "But the best part is that I decided if I wasn't afraid to be by myself when

I was five years old in a department store full of strangers, then I don't have to be afraid to be by myself today."

Andrea was no longer laughing. But she was grinning and giving Brenda the thumbs-up. When class was over and they had a chance to talk, Brenda found out that her breakthrough was also Andrea's. When Brenda suggested they go to the beach, Andrea could barely contain her enthusiasm.

Donna was already going to the beach club, so it was no problem convincing her to take Brenda and Andrea, too. They all pretended not to notice that David Silver sort of tagged along in the front seat.

Brenda and Andrea were very excited. After all, this trip to the beach club was a symbol of their having overcome their fears. Because Brenda wasn't afraid of being alone, she was no longer afraid of seeing Dylan. They could be *just friends*, and she would be fine. Evidently, Andrea felt the same way about her relationship with Brandon. If it was okay to be alone, then it was okay not to be half of a couple.

David disappeared as soon as they arrived, and Donna went off to see if she could find Kelly. Brenda and Andrea smiled weakly at each other. Brenda was still excited, but she was not as sure as she had been that coming here was a good idea.

And then the entire situation was out of her hands.

"Andrea!" called Brandon.

"Brenda!" called Dylan.

The boys were upon them, and there was no escape.

"We were just in the neighborhood," Brenda said.

"Yeah, right," Dylan said. He was not convinced.

"So," said Andrea as she glanced around. "This is the Beverly Hills Beach Club. It isn't nearly as tasteless and ostentatious as I would have expected."

Brandon laughed and hugged her, which took Andrea by surprise, but she didn't seem to mind.

Steve walked over to them grumbling to himself. He seemed monumentally bummed about something. He said, "This is the lowest. From here, I need a ladder to feel down."

"Tell all, dude," Brandon said.

"You remember Maia Landen?"

"The child vamp?"

"Yeah, well, she's obviously too young to have any taste in men. She wants to be 'my friend.'" Steve shuddered. "And you know who she's really fierce about? *Do you know?*"

"No, Steve, we don't," Brenda said sweetly.

At that moment, the worst possible thing

happened. David Silver walked by with his arm around the still-ravishing Maia. He punched Steve in the arm and asked, "Hey, big guy, what time do the grunion run tonight?"

David did not understand why this got a big laugh, but he was so entranced with Maia that he walked off with her and did not even ask what the problem was.

Brenda had never heard of grunion. Andrea had heard of them, but had never seen one.

"Nobody has," Brandon confided to Andrea.

Steve shot him a dirty look and said, "You'll see one tonight, trust me."

Brenda did not trust Steve any farther than she could throw him, but watching the sun set into the Pacific was a very enticing idea. The beach club emptied, and Brandon got out some blankets. The group strolled toward the ocean and made their camp just above the tide line, where the sand was dry.

Brenda sat down next to Dylan, but not actually touching him. The air was much cooler than it had been, almost cold, and she pulled a blanket around herself.

Brandon called out, "I'll bet there is no such thing as a grunion. Steve probably just made it up to lure babes to the beach."

There was general agreement, but Steve refused to be drawn out. He smiled and promised to have the last laugh.

As the sun set, it deepened from white to gold to orange, and soon it was gone. Brenda had not seen so many stars in the sky since she'd left Minnesota. The moon was a sliver of a boat on the horizon.

The whole setup was very romantic, though it was wasted on this group. Kelly refused to sit within arm's length of Steve, though their conversation was friendly enough. Brandon insisted on pretending that he and Andrea were just friends. Brenda loved Dylan, but things had been going too fast. Though with all her heart she wanted to touch him, and maybe do more than touch, she refused to allow herself to do it. She couldn't let that five-year-old Brenda be braver than the current Brenda was.

However, something strange and wonderful was happening between Donna and David, though neither of them would yet admit it. They made each other laugh, and Brenda caught them glancing at each other when one thought the other wouldn't notice. Very interesting. Donna had been alone too long. And David was nice enough, even if he *was* kind of a geek.

Brenda shivered and said, "You'd think they'd have the courtesy to show up at their own party."

"Like Brandon said," Dylan said, "grunion don't exist."

"Wait till next year," Steve said unhappily.

"Yeah," said Brandon, "but even without the grunion, it's really fine to see everybody."

"Almost everybody," Kelly said.

Brenda knew that Kelly was talking about David, but it seemed like a mean thing to say just at the moment.

Donna affectionately slugged David in the arm and said, "She's just kidding."

Brenda suspected that Kelly had not been kidding, but no more was said for a long time. The ocean bounded up to lick their toes, only to retreat and bound forward again. Where were the grunion?

5

The curse
of the McKays

THE GRUNION RAN AT LAST. MILLIONS OF
them flopped onto the shore, making the beach
froth with silver as far as Brenda could see.
Steve walked around, proud as if he'd invented
them.

Andrea kept saying with disbelief, "So those
are grunion, huh?"

The running of the grunion was the social
high point of Brenda's summer so far. Figuring
out what had happened at Dayton's Department
Store had been a triumph of sorts, but it was a
personal kind of thing and difficult to explain to
anyone else. Anyway, it was more of a school

thing than a summer thing. Brenda wasn't sure she wanted to find romance this summer (her relationship with Dylan had hardly been settled), but she wanted excitement of some sort. That was it: she wanted some nice nonthreatening summer excitement.

The next evening, Brenda was sitting in the living room feeling virtuous for watching the news on TV. Watching the news was not exactly a summer thing either. But nothing else was on and she was in the mood to watch *something*. She laid out newspaper on the coffee table and sorted the shells and smooth rocks she'd picked up on the beach that afternoon.

Soon, she would go upstairs and prepare for her dinner with Kelly. Kelly had told her that they would be eating somewhere special, to dress as if she were going to the theater or to a concert of classical music.

"What's up?" Brenda had asked.

"Important stuff. We must confer."

"About what?"

But Kelly refused to say any more, except that Brenda would be doing her a favor showing up, and that Brenda was not to worry about the expense of the dinner.

Brenda decided that Kelly would be telling her a secret about some guy. Only that kind of topic would be so important that it demanded a private dinner. Was she getting back together with Steve? Was she getting married? Had her protection failed her? Brenda's speculation was endlessly exciting, and knowing Kelly, the reality would be even more so.

Mr. Walsh ran around the house remembering things he needed to take with him on his business trip. It seemed that ever since the Walshes had moved to Beverly Hills, Mr. Walsh was always off somewhere else. Mr. Walsh was looking for his good blue shirt, and Brenda told him it was in the dirty clothes hamper because she'd worn it to the beach that day. He refused to understand why it was necessary for *Brenda* to wear his shirt.

"Guys like girls in guys' shirts," Brenda said.

Mrs. Walsh admitted it was true, and reminded Mr. Walsh of the times *she* had worn his shirts when they were first married. Mr. Walsh's face got red, and he said that he'd forgotten something upstairs, when the newscaster—who up to that moment had been talking about the politics of water—stopped him. She said, "And in other local news, Beverly Hills financier Jack McKay returned to the United States from Mexico today and was taken into the custody of federal marshals."

"My God," said Brenda. "That's Dylan's dad." While still holding a smooth rock, she turned up the sound. She'd known that Dylan's father had manipulated stocks in some illegal way, but to actually see him on TV, holding his handcuffed hands over his face, was shocking.

While the newscaster explained the exact nature of Mr. McKay's crime, Mr. Walsh said, "The smartest thing you ever did was break up with that crook."

With tears coming, Brenda said, "Dylan's not a crook, Daddy. And his father is innocent till proven guilty."

"Does he look innocent to you?" Mr. Walsh asked, and pointed at the TV screen.

Brenda couldn't stand her father's self-righteous attitude and she ran from the room. Upstairs, she flopped down on her bed and called the number of the McKay condo, where Dylan was staying. He was certain to be feeling awful about now. She had to comfort him. She didn't know what she would say, but she hoped she would think of something.

"Hi. This is Dylan. You know the drill. Leave your message at the beeperooni."

Brenda's disappointment that Dylan was not home became worry that he *was* home and that something terrible had happened to him. He'd given up drinking, but at a time like this, who knew what he'd do? The beep happened and Brenda said, "Dylan? Dylan, are you there? It's me, Brenda. If you're there, Dylan, please pick up." She waited, breathed into the hiss of the open line, and soon the machine at the other end clicked off.

"Oh, Dylan," Brenda said. She sat cross-legged on her bed, rocking up and back because there was nothing else to do.

When she looked up later, much time had passed. She would have to hurry if she wanted to be dressed properly when Kelly called to pick her up. She chose a suit of conservative cut, and spent some time with her makeup. Kelly was always very stylish, but rarely extreme, and Brenda felt that she could be no less classy.

Kelly honked outside, and Brenda ran down the stairs. "School tomorrow," Mrs. Walsh called after her.

"I'll be home before midnight," Brenda called.

"Eleven!"

"Eleven-thirty!"

And then Brenda was out the door. She climbed into the red BMW and Kelly drove away. Kelly would never be anything less than pretty, but at the moment she was very serious.

"So, Kelly," Brenda said.

"So, Brenda."

When Kelly continued to drive without speaking, Brenda said, "This mysterioso thing is killing me, Kel. I have enough on my mind with Dylan and his father."

"Yeah, I heard about it on the radio. How's

Dylan doing?"

"I don't know. He won't answer his phone." Brenda jumbled her hands in her lap and looked out the window at the passing lights. "But we're not here to talk about me and Dylan."

"No," said Kelly. "If we were, *you'd* be buying dinner."

"Yeah," said Brenda, "at the Peach Pit."

"I promised to tell you over dinner," Kelly said, and for the next fifteen minutes did nothing but drive.

Kelly took them to Enyart's, a long low restaurant on Sunset. If you didn't know where to look, you'd never find it. Which was the way the management liked it, Brenda supposed. They left the car with a very cute parking attendant and walked inside. The place was bright and noisy and decorated in the latest industrial fashion: the pink walls were crossed by gray air-conditioning ducts.

Kelly had a reservation, and a woman took them to a table under a painting of black and red blotches. She asked them if they wanted drinks. Did the woman really think they were eighteen, or would she ask for ID if they ordered alcohol? Brenda decided to avoid the possible embarrassment and ordered ginger ale, which would be sophisticated without being alcoholic. Evidently, Kelly had come to the same conclusion because she ordered a cola.

"Now," said Brenda, and stared at Kelly.

Kelly fidgeted for a moment and then said, "Something happened this summer."

"I hope you know a good doctor," Brenda said, only half kidding.

"No. Nothing like that."

Kelly really looked uncomfortable, leading Brenda to believe that whatever she had to talk about was no joking matter. A waiter brought them their drinks. He was a dark handsome guy who might have been as old as thirty. He had a British accent, which Brenda always went wild over. But she controlled herself. They were not here to meet guys. Brenda blanched when she saw the prices on the menu, and she whispered to Kelly, "Are you sure you want to do this?"

"Just *order*, Brenda. It's the plastic's party."

The waiter smiled.

Kelly and Brenda both ordered the poached salmon and the waiter went away.

Kelly said, "Last week Mom and I were at the beach."

Brenda nodded. Kelly's mom, Jackie, was very hip and cute for a mom. She was a short blonde who shared clothes up and back with Kelly. Brenda could not imagine dressing out of her own mom's closet, but in the case of Kelly and her mom, it worked to the advantage of both of them.

"Your mom's getting married."

"I'm not playing Twenty Questions, Brenda. Do you want to hear this or not?"

"Sorry."

"Anyway, we were at the beach. Since she stopped drinking, she's been getting out a lot more. She thought that without a margarita in her hand, she'd be totally bored, but I pointed out the scenery, and that perked her right up."

"Scenery? Men?"

"What else? Anyway, I pointed out a particular guy to her. At first, she thought I was talking about Steve—"

"Steve!" Brenda said, amazed.

"Chill out, Brenda. I wasn't. I was talking about a guy named Kyle Conners. He is absolutely awesome, and I don't mean his volleyball playing, although that's awesome, too."

"I've seen him around. I didn't think he was your type." Kyle was muscular enough, and had a nice smile, but Brenda thought he was short and a little on the slim side.

"He is *definitely* my type. And the fact that Steve was jealous was kind of a bonus. Steve thinks he is God's gift to volleyball."

"Among other things."

"Yeah. Among other things. So Kyle serves the ball, Steve glances in my direction and the ball hits him in the head. It bounces off his head and rolls over to where I'm standing."

"Luck?"

"Skill. I pick up the ball and Kyle comes to get it. I ask him for private lessons."

"How private?"

"Private enough. We were on the beach almost before the sea gulls. Anyway, Steve's watching me talk to Kyle, and I can see the steam coming out of his ears."

The fish came, and for a while Kelly said no more. The flavor made Brenda's mouth light up. Though she was eager to hear Kelly's next installment, Brenda tried not to bolt her food.

At school the next day, Brenda discovered that Andrea's usual journalistic curiosity had hooked onto Mr. McKay and his legal troubles. Brenda didn't want to talk about the situation, but Andrea was persistent.

"Will he post bond?"

"Andrea, I don't know any more about it than you do. Less maybe, since you probably read the paper this morning."

"Don't you talk to Dylan?"

"We broke up, remember?"

"But still, at a time like this—"

"If Dylan wants to talk to me, he knows the phone rings at my end, too." Brenda escaped into the drama classroom. She liked Andrea, but Andrea could be a real pest sometimes.

Someone ought to give her the lecture about the public's right to know needing to be balanced with the right of personal privacy.

David Silver was talking to Donna at the other side of the room. She could do both herself and Donna a favor by going over to talk to her. David backed away, and Andrea seemed to have gotten Brenda's message, because she didn't bother her again about Dylan's dad.

Mr. Suiter was sitting behind his desk reading from a big book, what some people called a tome. When the bell rang, he hefted the book in one hand like a weight, and sat on the front edge of his desk talking about William Shakespeare.

Donna whispered to Brenda, "Shakespeare? I thought this class was supposed to be fun."

"Shakespeare's first big hit was *Henry the Sixth*. He followed it with a sequel. Does anybody know what the sequel was called?"

One hand went up. Mr. Suiter ignored Andrea and called on Donna. Brenda's blood ran cold on her behalf.

Donna looked around wildly, and said, "Uh, *Henry the Sixth, Part Two*?"

Everybody laughed. Donna could be a dear thing, but she was not exactly strong in the academics department.

Mr. Suiter surprised everybody when he said, "She's right!"

Donna smiled and tried to pretend she'd

known it all the time.

"And to honor Shakespeare, the Bard of Avon, a better playwright even than Neil Simon, we're going to try some scenes from his plays."

Everybody but Donna groaned. Still high from her victory, she said, "Great! Shakespeare! Wow!"

"*Hamlet* was good enough for Mel Gibson, but we're going to try something a little closer to the hearts of high school kids than the assassination of kings. Love, romance, violence, intrigue, maybe even a little sex."

"I didn't know Shakespeare wrote *Raiders of the Lost Ark*," David said.

Mr. Suiter spoke right through the class' laughter. "No. I mean the original of *West Side Story: Romeo and Juliet.* The question is, which of you ingenues wants to play the ultimate teen queen?"

Brenda thought she'd make a great Juliet, and she could see that every other girl in the class was thinking the same thing. They all wanted to, but like Brenda, none of them were certain enough of their acting skills to volunteer.

"Donna? How about you?"

Before Donna had a chance to protest, Mr. Suiter was on to something else. "Now, for your partner, the biggest teen heartthrob of all time." He looked into the eyes of every guy in class. Brenda had never heard that room so quiet. At last, Mr. Suiter quoth, "Never was there a story of more woe than this of Donna and her Romeo." His hand felt onto David Siiver's shoulder.

Donna's eyes got big, and she made a small sound of surprise. David smiled, and waved at her.

Well, Brenda thought, you couldn't say Mr. Suiter didn't have unusual ideas about casting.

They went on with the exercises they'd started the day before, but it was obvious to Brenda that the minds of Mr. Suiter's students were on *Romeo and Juliet.* David continued to grin, and he hung around Donna even more than usual. During the break, he proposed that he and Donna get together and rehearse. Donna responded as if he'd suggested they get together and wrestle alligators. Donna finally shook David off by promising that they would rehearse RSN, or "real soon now."

Donna drove Andrea to Brenda's house, and from there, they were going to hit the beach. But they took some time to sit eating ice cream in the Walsh kitchen while Mrs. Walsh cleaned her sink and reminisced about her own experiences with Shakespeare. The other girls listened eagerly, but Brenda could not help being a little embarrassed.

"I was Lady Macbeth in the class play," Mrs. Walsh said.

"You weren't," Brenda said. This was the first she'd heard of her mother *ever* acting. She had trouble believing her mother had even gone to school.

Mrs. Walsh poured a little cleanser on a spot in the sink and rubbed it hard while she said, "'Out damned spot! Out I say!' . . . Who would have thought the old sink to have had so much dirt in it?"

Brenda didn't know what to make of that, and evidently Donna didn't either. Was her mom quoting Shakespeare or had her mind suddenly snapped? Andrea laughed. Had Andrea's mind snapped, too?

Mrs. Walsh said, "It was a joke. *Macbeth,* act five, scene one."

Andrea said, "You see, Macbeth had just murdered the king, and there's all this blood—"

The ringing of the telephone saved them from having to listen to the remainder of Andrea's explanation. With more than normal enthusiasm, Brenda answered it.

"Hello, is Brandon Walsh there?"

"Brandon's not here right now. Can I take a message?"

"This is Malibu Hospital. Please tell him that Dylan McKay has had a surfing accident."

"Dylan?"

"Yes, Dylan McKay. Will you give Mr. Walsh the message?"

"Oh, my God! What happened?"

Questions exploded in the kitchen and Brenda shushed them all while she strained to hear the woman at the other end of the line. "We're not sure, but he's resting comfortably. Are you his sister?"

"No," Brenda said. "Just a friend." She hung up and, in a dead voice, repeated the message.

"Is he all right?" Andrea asked.

"I don't know. They said he's resting comfortably."

Mrs. Walsh rinsed her hands, wiped them, and said, "Let's go."

Brenda could not help thinking that she should have loved Dylan more when she had the chance.

6

Is there a doctor in the house?

DONNA FELT THAT DYLAN'S INJURY WAS somehow a family event, and that she shouldn't intrude.

"But they're not his family either," Andrea cried as Donna dragged her away.

"Come on, Andrea, I'll drive you home."

Brenda and her mother were out the door right behind them. To Brenda, it seemed that Mrs. Walsh had never driven so slowly. Brenda bounced like an excited kid on the seat next to her.

"You don't want me to get a ticket at a time like this, do you, Brenda?"

"I suppose not." Brenda got a grip on herself.

They found a place to park and ran in at the emergency entrance. The nurses and doctors were busy with a young guy who'd been knifed, and it took awhile before anyone even noticed Brenda and her mother were there.

When Brenda finally got their attention, she was directed to a Dr. Silverstein, who seemed a little distracted as she found the right chart and reported that Dylan had been unconscious when he'd been brought in, but he had only a mild concussion and a few cracked ribs.

"Can I see him?"

"Are you family?" Dr. Silverstein asked.

Brenda didn't see that that was any of the doctor's business. "Er, I'm the closest thing he has at the moment."

Dr. Silverstein studied her and then said, "All right. Room twenty-seven. Don't stay long. He needs his rest."

Dreading the meeting before her, Brenda walked down the hallway. Most doors were open, allowing her a view of pain, suffering, and weird machinery. Strange chemical odors floated by. Orderlies hurried along pushing carts loaded with stuff that belonged in Dr. Frankenstein's lab. Brenda knew hospitals were necessary, but she really hated visiting them.

In room 27, Brenda found Dylan lying in bed

with his eyes closed, and with bandages wrapped around his head and chest. Would he awaken? Would he remember her? He looked very sweet and vulnerable, but was anybody home? She rested her hand on the rail at the foot of Dylan's bed and his eyes fluttered open. He smiled like a sleepy young child and said, "I must be dreaming. I'm seeing angels."

"Dylan, it's me, Brenda."

"Brenda?"

Oh, God. "You remember me, don't you, Dylan?"

"Of course I remember you. How did you know I was here?"

"The hospital found Brandon's name and number in your pocket. Oh, Dylan, you scared me."

"I'm fine." He smiled. "It was awesome."

"Awesome, my foot. You're lucky to be alive." This was no time for her to be giving him a lecture on water safety. She asked, "Does your father know you're here?"

"I guess. His lawyer was here. Someone had to give them permission to treat me."

She moved to touch his hand. It seemed too warm. "Everything's going to be okay. You're going to be out of here in no time." She looked out the door. Mom was waiting for her back in the waiting room. Dylan should probably be sleeping. "I better go."

"Don't leave." His hand tightened around hers, but without strength.

"The doctor says you need to rest." She kissed him on the bandages that crossed his forehead, and walked out before he asked her to stay again. She wouldn't be able to leave if he did that.

In the waiting room, Mrs. Walsh stood and said, "How is he?"

"Okay, I guess, for a guy who's just come in second in a misunderstanding with the ocean."

"The doctors wanted to keep him here for a few days because he has no one at home to take care of him. But I told them we'd take Dylan home with us."

Brenda was stunned. She could not be hearing this. "Mom, Dylan can't live in our house. He and I broke up."

"We can't just leave him here, Brenda. Besides, he's Brandon's friend, too."

"I don't get it, Mom. First, you and Dad order me not even to see him, and then you tuck him into the room next to mine. This, as Andrea would say, is craziness!"

"It's just for a few days."

"What will Dad say?"

Mrs. Walsh bit her lip and said, "Dad will understand that Dylan is a friend who needs our help."

"Yeah, right."

It seemed so simple to Brenda, yet her mom refused to understand. They wheeled Dylan out to the car, and with the help of a couple of nurses, got him into the back seat. Brenda sat in front.

Dylan didn't say much during the ride because he was full of painkillers. At home, Brenda helped her mom get Dylan upstairs one painful step at a time, and into Brandon's room.

But Brenda drew the line at serving Dylan dinner. It was tough enough ignoring Dylan when he wasn't around. Brenda refused to force herself into his face, or him into hers. She said, "This was *your* idea, Mom. I won't play Nancy Nurse." She went outside before her mother could answer. It was a beautiful night. Why not go outside? The chill Brenda felt must have been coming from inside her.

Brandon had to argue awhile before he could convince Dylan he didn't mind sleeping on the couch. He was loading up with towels and blankets when he asked Dylan, "So, what happened out there?"

Dylan shook his head. "I pulled a real gremmie, you know? The tube closed out on me and I got whomped from behind. Instant wipeout. I should have seen it coming."

"I guess you had other things on your mind."

"This has nothing to do with my father, Dr. Sigmund Walsh."

Mrs. Walsh knocked and came in bearing a tray arranged like a work of art. The smell would make a stone hungry. She set the tray across Dylan's legs and announced, "Roast chicken with rosemary, broccoli au gratin, new potatoes, and chocolate mousse cake for dessert."

"Wow," said Dylan.

"Yeah, wow," Brandon said. Dylan was discovering the up side to being an invalid in the Walsh house.

Dylan picked up a fork, and waved it over the plate, looking for the right place to dig in. He said, "Is Brenda around?"

Hesitantly, Mrs. Walsh said, "I think she went out."

"You wouldn't call her stubborn, would you?" Dylan asked.

Mrs. Walsh put her hand to her chest, feigned shock, and said, "Brenda? Stubborn? Impossible."

The laugh cost Dylan some pain. But he came out of it with a pretty speech thanking Mrs. Walsh for everything. "A guy forgets what it's like to have a real family."

"That's okay," Brandon said. "She can't help herself. Suffering brings out the mother hen in her."

She patted Dylan's hand, ordered him to get better, and left the two alone. Dylan took a bite of chicken. Around it, he asked, "What about the papa rooster?"

"Dad? He's cool."

"Brandon, your dad's a lot of things, but cool is not one of them."

"Mom will deal with Dad. You just get better." Brandon took his linen and walked out of the room before he needed to have an argument with Dylan about that, too.

As he passed his parents' bedroom, he heard his mother's half of a conversation that had to be with Dad. "I don't need to lock her door. Dylan can't even move." The conversation continued, but Brandon didn't need to hear any more of it. Mom could handle Dad for the moment. But as he continued down the hall, Brandon wondered what would happen in a day or two when Dad got home.

Brandon was reading on the couch when he heard Brenda come in. He waited for bathroom noises to stop, and for the sound of her footsteps to return to her bedroom. Then he went upstairs to talk with her. He wasn't sure he was doing the right thing, but for Dylan's sake, for the sake of peace in the house, he had to do something.

He found Brenda reading on her bed. From the doorway, it looked like Shakespeare, some play in verse. To let her know he was there, he said, "The play's the thing, huh, Bren?"

"*Hamlet.* I'm going to do Ophelia in class."

Just dive in, Brandon told himself. "He's been here all day and you haven't said a word to him."

"I'm not sure I can stay 'just friends' with Dylan, Brandon. Not while he's here in this house."

At least she hadn't said, *him who*? "Just talk to him, Brenda. Say good night or something."

She rolled over and glared at Brandon. "This is none of your business, Brandon. It's between me and Dylan."

Brenda ran so true to form that Brandon had to smile. "He's right. You really are stubborn."

Brenda knew she was not stubborn, and she would tell Dylan so. She whipped on her bathrobe and stomped down the hall. The door to Brandon's room was open, and she stood in the doorway looking angrily at Dylan. "I am *not* stubborn."

"Good evening to you, too. Come on in."

"No."

"Are you avoiding me?"

She was, of course, but to prove to herself that she was not, she walked into the room and sat at the foot of the bed. "I made a promise to myself, Dylan. I need this time to straighten things out in my own head."

"I can't get through this without you, Bren. You're the only person I can trust." He took her wrist and pulled her toward him. She wanted to resist, but found herself unable to. She wanted to ask him whether he meant he couldn't get through recuperating from his injury, or enduring his father's legal problems, but she decided the difference in this case was irrelevant. Her mouth was only inches from his. They kissed softly. She pulled away from him and took a deep breath as she stood.

"I'm sorry, Dylan. I really am. But I can't."

"Can't what?"

Good question. Brenda said, "This. Any of this."

Feeling both noble and like a fool, she walked away from Dylan, down the hall and back to her own room, where she turned off the light and tried to sleep. But Dylan's face rose through the dream-murk, and tempted her. She hadn't even figured out life yet. It wasn't fair that she should also be a teenager in love. One or the other, but both together was a heavy burden.

She awoke with a start, having to go to the bathroom. She looked at the lighted dial of her bedside clock and saw that she had actually slept for some hours. It was after midnight, and

"The boys of summer." From left to right: Jason Priestley, Luke Perry, Ian Ziering. Kneeling: Brian Austin Green.

Shannen Doherty
as Brenda Walsh.

Jennie Garth as
Kelly Taylor.

"The dynamic duo." Luke Perry as Dylan McKay and Jason Priestley as Brandon Walsh.

Tori Spelling as the
ever fashionable
Donna Martin.

Gabrielle Carteris as
the intellectual Andrea
Zuckerman.

Luke Perry as Dylan McKay and Shannen Doherty as Brenda Walsh.

Ian Ziering as Steve Sanders and Jason Priestley as Brandon Walsh.

Jennie Garth and Shannen Doherty find a new friend on the beach.

Luke Perry as the intriguing character of Dylan McKay.

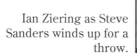

Ian Ziering as Steve Sanders winds up for a throw.

The gang of West Beverly High - *From left to right:* Brian Austin Green, Tori Spelling, Luke Perry, Shannen Doherty, Jason Priestley, Gabrielle Carteris, Jennie Garth, and Ian Ziering.

the air that drifted in through her open window was soft and cool and smelled of night-blooming flowers. Crickets chirped. A perfect night for love, damn it.

Could she safely go to the bathroom? What if she met Dylan? So what? It was her bathroom. And she could handle him. The problem was handling herself. So, it was kind of a test, going to the bathroom. And after all, she might not run into him. Which would be a disappointment, actually. She got up and headed for the bathroom.

She opened the door and saw the door across from her open. Dylan's crooked shape leaned against the door frame. They said some stupid stuff to each other; each offered to let the other go first. What Brenda really wanted to do was take Dylan in her arms, kiss him, make love to him, make him all better.

What she said was, "You go first. You're already here, and it's hard for you to move around."

"Thanks."

Brenda backed out of the bathroom, and leaned against the closed door breathing hard. And then, embarrassed by the noises she heard, she went back to bed and waited for her turn.

The next day, Brenda felt more ready than ever to perform Ophelia in drama class. She concentrated, shut out the traffic noise, the tapping of the blinds against the windows, her own breathing, and with some passion she spoke Shakespeare's words:

And I, of ladies most deject and wretched,
That suck'd the honey of his music vows,
Now see that noble and most sovereign reason,
Like sweet bells jangled, out of tune and harsh;
That unmatch'd form and feature of blown youth
Blasted with ecstasy: O, woe is me,
To have seen what I have seen, see what I see!

Mr. Suiter led the big applause that followed her performance. He complimented her on really understanding Ophelia, who more than anything else, was confused by Hamlet's actions. Talk about confusion! The reason Brenda understood Ophelia's feelings so well was because she was sharing a bathroom with Hamlet. Was Dylan crazy? Was she? Brenda really didn't know.

The bell rang, and Mr. Suiter reminded them that at their next meeting David and Donna would perform a scene from *Romeo and Juliet.*

"Are you guys ready?" he asked.

They smiled, but the smiles looked a little forced. Brenda suspected that one way or the other, whatever David and Donna worked out would be pretty entertaining, if not exactly what Shakespeare had in mind.

On the bus home from school, Brenda practiced how to act with Dylan. She tried a number of approaches; at last she decided to be friendly but a little aloof; anything warmer would certainly lead her into a messy romantic quagmire that she simply was not ready to explore. Sex could lead only to harder stuff.

When she got home and called out to her mother, Dylan answered, "Your mom's out shopping."

Trouble was coming, Brenda knew, but she saw no way to avoid it. To ignore Dylan would be rude if they were the only two people in the house. Besides, she wanted to try out her new attitude. She walked into the living room and Dylan said, "Nobody's here but me and Oprah." He fired the remote and the TV went off. The silence was deadly.

"Can I get you anything?" Brenda asked. "A soda or something?"

Dylan smiled and said, "That would be great. Thanks."

While Brenda walked to the kitchen, Dylan called after her, "Your mom said some sandwiches are on a plate in the fridge."

"Okay."

She found them, grabbed a soda, and was on her way back, when Dylan called, "And an apple, okay?"

"Okay." She took one from the bowl on the

dining-room table and walked into the living room feeling a little put upon, which was silly. She'd asked him if she could do anything for him. "Is that it?" She set down the sandwich plate, the apple, and the cold can of soda.

"Maybe that blanket over there." Dylan pointed.

Brenda got it for him from the back of a chair, but she was starting to fume.

"Oh, and I left my book on that table over there."

If he thought she was Nancy Nurse, he was sadly mistaken. With an edge in her voice, Brenda asked, "Does Master Dylan wish anything else?"

"There is one more thing."

"Yes?"

"I want you."

Dylan smiled and the ice that had been forming inside Brenda melted. How could she not love this guy? She had been holding back too long. She ran across the room to his couch of pain and lay across him.

Dylan grunted and said, "Watch it."

"Sorry," Brenda said, and pulled away.

"No. Don't leave."

She kissed his warm mouth and felt his arms pulling her closer. His broken ribs made things difficult, but they persisted. Brenda said, "Staying away from you is the hardest thing I've ever done."

Brenda was lost in her happiness at being near Dylan again. Dylan occasionally flinched with pain, but he would not let her go.

"What the hell's going on here?"

A shower of cold water could not have broken her mood more quickly or completely. She jumped away from Dylan and said the first thing that came into her head. "Daddy, it's not what you think!"

Mr. Walsh stood in the middle of the living room with his suitcase in one hand and a laptop computer in the other. He was very angry.

7

Parts unknown

BRENDA AND DYLAN HAD ONLY BEEN kissing, she knew that. And yet, now that her head was clearing, Brenda felt that she had somehow betrayed a trust, not only of her parents but of herself. Which was silly. Nothing wrong had happened here. They had only been kissing. Surely her father knew that high school kids kissed. Surely, he relied on her to know *who* to kiss.

Evidently not. She could read the expression on Mr. Walsh's face. He was taking in the spectacle of his only daughter being mauled by some juvenile delinquent who had somehow tricked his way into the bosom of the

Walsh family. In his anger, Mr. Walsh had forgotten to set down his luggage. He said, "It isn't what I think, Brenda? Then please tell me what it is."

"I can explain, Mister Walsh," Dylan said.

"There's nothing to explain. Except maybe why you decided to abuse our hospitality by taking advantage of my daughter."

The guy lived in the Stone Age, Brenda thought. "Daddy, it wasn't like that!"

But he refused to listen. He marched stiffly upstairs leaving Brenda and Dylan at opposite ends of the couch. The couch might as well have been a continent. Brenda kept saying she was sorry, and Dylan kept telling her not to worry.

When Mrs. Walsh came home, Brenda pleaded with her to talk to Dad. Mrs. Walsh glanced at Dylan, and then went up the stairs, very worried.

The door to her parents' bedroom closed, and Brenda crept up the stairs. She sat on the top step with Dylan a step beneath her. They did not have to listen at keyholes to find out what Mr. and Mrs. Walsh were discussing. The argument filled the house.

Mr. Walsh was of the opinion that he had saved his daughter from a fate worse than death by coming home from his business trip when he did.

Mrs. Walsh's more liberal view was that her husband was overreacting, and that they had to trust Brenda.

Mr. Walsh trusted Brenda, but not with Dylan around. He would not kick an invalid into the street, but he wanted Dylan gone as soon as possible.

"I'm sorry," Brenda whispered.

"Not your fault, Bren," Dylan said.

Dinner that evening was layered with large cool silences. Conversation was limited to requests that something be passed, followed by a polite acknowledgment. If Brandon had been there, the meal might have gone more smoothly, but he was working late at the beach club.

Immediately after dinner, Dylan went to Brandon's room, and Brenda went to her room. Well, she hoped her father was satisfied. Instead of acting like civilized adults, each of them was locked into their own box. She read *Romeo and Juliet* until her eyes watered when she thought about how difficult love was. Wherefore art thou, Dylan? Brenda was pretty sure the problem was not who Dylan was or even who his father was. As far as Mr. Walsh was concerned, the fact that Dylan was a guy who was interested in his daughter, was bad enough.

Brenda slept through the night with no dreams or bathroom adventures.

The next morning, Brenda found a note by her bed. It was from Dylan. He thanked her for everything, asked her to pass his thanks on to her mom, and told her he didn't want to be a burden anymore. He was leaving. Parts unknown. Love, Dylan.

Brenda started to read the note again, but began to cry so hard she couldn't finish it. Where would Dylan go? He didn't have any money. He must be in pain even shifting the gears of his Porsche. He could end up in a gutter somewhere.

Brenda had to do something. She had to find him and bring him back. She didn't know how, but maybe that wasn't important. She just couldn't stay under the same roof as the guy who'd thrown Dylan into the street.

With the note still in her hand, she ran downstairs and found her parents in the kitchen drinking coffee as if nothing were wrong. She threw the note on the counter. Her mother picked it up and untwisted it.

"Dylan's gone," Mrs. Walsh said.

"What?" Mr. Walsh said.

"I hope you're happy now," Brenda said as she headed for the door.

"Where are you going?" Mr. Walsh asked. His voice had an edge. Was it anger or concern? Brenda didn't much care.

"I'm going to find him. And when I do, I'm

going to apologize for having such a jerk for a father."

As she slammed the door behind her, she was immediately sorry she'd called her father a jerk. He wasn't so much a jerk, actually, as a man with strong stupid principles.

Relationships were a bitch. Romeo and Juliet, Dylan and Brenda, Kyle and Kelly. Kelly's relationship with Kyle was a lot more unusual than Brenda's with Dylan and the problems were entirely different.

Kelly had said that she'd asked Kyle for private lessons and then the poached salmon had come. It had been very good, but Brenda had rushed a little, hoping that when she finished, Kelly would continue her story.

They'd had a few bites, and evidently, Kelly couldn't stand keeping her story in anymore.

Enyart's became more crowded as Brenda and Kelly ate. It was a happening place and the noise was very exciting. Still, in their little corner, Brenda felt as if she and Kelly were alone.

"So, you were up with the sea gulls," Brenda said. "What happened at the lesson?"

"At first, not much. Just volleyball."

"How disappointing for you," Brenda said.

"Not entirely. For one thing, my game actually *did* improve. And once, I hit the ball funny and hurt my wrist. He rubbed it for me." Kelly looked at Brenda meaningfully. "He has *very* nice hands."

"Okay. He's the 'nice hands' poster child."

Kelly smiled as if lost for a moment in memory. She said, "And then at last, he asked me for a date. Steve saw us and bothered to give me the bulletin that Kyle has a girlfriend. Now, this is really good. When Steve gave me the bulletin, I called him a jerk, and he said that Kyle was just playing with my mind. So I said, 'Well, that would be a welcome change, wouldn't it?'"

"Left him in the dust," Brenda said appreciatively.

"Right. But it turned out Steve was right. Or at least I thought so for a while."

Kelly picked up a flake of salmon and chewed on it so long that Brenda had to ask, "So did the date happen or what?"

"It happened, all right. But not the way I expected. We had a picnic on the beach. Sand got in everywhere."

"Everywhere?"

"Almost everywhere. Anyway, we huddled around the campfire, though to tell the truth, it wasn't very cold. Kyle was being very sweet and I went a little crazy."

"Sounds good to me. I'll bet it sounded good to Kyle, too."

"That was the surprise. I ran toward the

water throwing my clothes in all directions, you know, so we could skinny-dip? Kyle couldn't get into it."

"Imagine that. A man without hormones."

"He wouldn't even kiss me. He started, and we were going pretty good, and then he backed away as if he was embarrassed or something."

"Kelly Taylor losing her touch?"

"My touch or worse. I was really upset, and I felt like a fool. I'd never been rejected like that, not even before I had my nose done. I asked him to take me home and he did. We didn't even talk the whole way."

"So he really was playing mind games."

"That's what I thought. The next day I saw Steve ragging on him, and Kyle tried to pretend that we'd had a great time. Then Kyle had the nerve to tell me we needed to talk. I just walked away. Steve asked me in his nastiest possible voice if my summer fling was over. You can imagine the kind of mood I was in."

"Just one guy," Brenda said gently. "I feel better knowing you're human like the rest of us."

"Glad to hear it. But that isn't the end of the story."

"No?"

"No. Are you done with the salmon? Let's get that dessert cart over here. I feel like spending some calories, and this is the place for it."

■ ■ ■

When Brenda came back to the house a few hours after finding Dylan's note, she decided to do something constructive for a change. She called Mr. McKay's condo and the Bel Age Hotel, where Mr. McKay maintained a suite. Nobody had seen Dylan, or even knew he'd been hurt. Brenda spent too much time bringing the curious up to speed on him.

The minute Brenda got off the phone it rang, and Mrs. Walsh leaped to answer it. "Probably the only chance I'll have to talk on my own phone until we find Dylan."

She got serious, admitted that she was Mrs. Walsh, and then told somebody at the other end that she didn't know where Dylan was. "He is?" "He was?" "He did?" "He didn't!"

When Mrs. Walsh hung up, she asked Brenda if she knew anything about Dylan going to Hawaii to see his mother.

"Hawaii? Mother? Who was that?"

"That was Mr. McKay's lawyer. She got our number from Malibu Hospital. It seems that when Mr. McKay turned himself in, Dylan's mother made arrangements for Dylan to come stay with her in Hawaii. The morning of the accident, he was supposed to be on a plane."

"But he went surfing instead."

"Right. And now nobody knows where he is."

"If Daddy wasn't such a jerk—"

"Your father is not a jerk, and I don't want to hear that kind of talk again." Mrs. Walsh put her hand tenderly on Brenda's shoulder. "He just has a very short fuse when it comes to his daughter."

"I know, Mom."

Brenda knew her father wasn't a jerk, but she also knew that nobody had seen Dylan since yesterday evening. How could she sleep when he was out there on the street?

The elements seemed to understand how upset Brenda was because that night, warm wind blew in from the desert, shoving palm leaves along the street like boats, and making everybody feel anxious. Raymond Chandler had called this red wind, a time when anything could happen. She fell asleep listening to the telephone cable slap against the side of the house.

The next morning the wind was gone, but it had left behind piles of leaves, broken tree limbs, and the cleanest air Brenda had ever inhaled, cleaner even than the stuff back in Minnesota. She could actually see the Hollywood Hills.

At school, Donna admitted to Brenda that neither she nor David were very good actors. This did not seem to be much of a problem compared to Brenda's worries about Dylan, but she made polite noises. Brenda said, "It's only a summer school drama class. The grade can't mean much."

"Maybe not, but David came up with a way for us to get an A apiece."

"That's great. What are you going to do?"

Donna smiled smugly and said, "You'll have to wait and see."

Waiting to see was fine with Brenda. Where was Dylan?

Because of the red wind, Brandon had a lot of extra work to do when he got to the beach club. A couple of garbage bags had been tossed around, and trash from the day before was all over the place. The gardeners were going to have a hell of a job, too. Leaves and branches were everywhere.

Brandon found the door of a cabana open, and he went to close it. He checked inside to make sure nothing had blown over, and got the shock of his life. Dylan was curled up on the sofa.

"Hey, man," Brandon called.

Dylan opened his eyes, and struggled to a sitting position. His ribs were obviously still tender.

"What are you doing here, man? Everybody's out looking for you."

"Needed a place to crash."

"Well, you can't stay here. Henry'll call the

police." It seemed unlikely that Henry would do
such a thing to Dylan, but he wouldn't be happy
either. Dylan couldn't stay here.

Working hard, Dylan got to his feet and had
Brandon help him move a small dresser. Behind it,
Dylan pointed out a row of horizontal dents in the
molding, starting at about two feet off the ground
and rising by increments to about four feet.

"What are you showing me here?"

"Those marks show how I grew. The beach
club painted out the dates."

"This is your family's cabana!"

"Right. We spent every summer here till I
was six and my parents broke up. That's where
the marks stop." He touched them gently. "We
had a good time. My dad used to toss me in the
air and catch me. He told me he'd never drop
me, never let me fall. Now he's dropped me, big
time. And it looks as if everybody else has, too."

"Dylan—"

"Next thing you know, I'll be living on Skid
Drive."

"Where's that?"

"That's where all the bums in Beverly Hills
hang out."

Brandon must have looked as bewildered as
he felt because Dylan said, "Don't worry, bro.
It's just a joke. A bad joke." As his eyes swept
the room, Dylan said, "A guided tour of the
memory cabana."

Dylan really looked terrible. Maybe he'd slept but he hadn't rested. Brandon said, "How about breakfast?"

Dylan rubbed his hands together while he looked at the floor.

"I'm buying," Brandon said.

"Your family's been buying all week."

"Okay. If you're not hungry," Brandon said, and turned to leave.

"I'll pay you back, I swear."

The beach club restaurant wasn't open yet, but Brandon had friends on the staff, so a few minutes later, he and Dylan were scarfing up eggs, bacon, toast, and coffee.

Brandon said, "So, why weren't you on that plane to Hawaii?"

Dylan's fork stopped in midair and he said, "How did you know about that?"

"My mom talked to the lawyer." After a sip of coffee, Brandon said, "*Your* mom is worried about you."

"If she *is* worried, she's probably taking care of it by aligning her crystals or rubbing my baby pictures with yak fat or something."

"Huh?"

"My mom's a flake. Except for having to put up with her spaced-out phone calls in the middle of the night, I don't have much to do with her. And I like it that way."

"Sooner or later, you'll have to see her,

Dylan. You can't avoid your mother forever."

"I can try," Dylan said as he chased egg yoke with a wedge of toast.

The guy was cutting himself off from everything. Brandon couldn't let this happen. Dylan might really end up on Skid Drive, or wherever. Brandon said, "Let me talk to Dad. He'll let you come back."

"Forget it. He threw me out."

"He says a lot of silly things when he's angry."

Dylan watched Brandon for a moment and then shrugged. "Talk to him if you want. It won't do any good."

"It better do some good or Brenda will never forgive any of us."

While Brandon and Dylan were having breakfast, Brenda and her father were doing the same. They ostentatiously did not speak with each other. The tension was terrible and Brenda thought that if only her father were a little less stubborn, a little less protective, none of this would have happened.

The phone rang once and Brenda answered it. It was Brandon telling her that Dylan was all right. Brenda was delighted, of course, but for her father's benefit, she tried not to show it. Why should she let him off the hook so easily?

Brenda said, "Thank you," and hung up.

"Who was it?"

"A friend. No big deal."

When Brenda finished her bowl of fruit, she put it into the dishwasher. Her father came up behind her with his coffee cup and said, "How many times do I have to tell you? Bowls go with the bowls."

"I know how to load a dishwasher."

In his eagerness to get to the dishwasher and demonstrate, Mr. Walsh forced Brenda aside and began rearranging things. The crockery rang as Mr. Walsh moved things around. "The dinner plates with the dinner plates. That way you get more in. Come on, Brenda. There's a right way and a wrong way."

Brenda was so tense with anger she could not move. This argument was not about dishes, and they both knew it. She said, "And then there's the Walsh way, right, Dad?"

Mr. Walsh turned slowly to look at her with great seriousness.

Brenda felt like an insect pinned to a card. She didn't know what her father would say next, but she suspected she wouldn't like it.

8

Handprints

UNEXPECTEDLY, MR. WALSH SMILED, throwing Brenda off her stride. She'd expected more anger, a patronizing explanation, but not a smile. She was a sucker for her dad's smiles. Even in the heat of an argument, she could not help liking him when he smiled.

Mr. Walsh closed the dishwasher and said, "So far, the Walsh way's worked pretty well, at least when it comes to raising kids."

Brenda did her best to stay angry. "Maybe Brandon and I are done being raised."

"Oh, you think so, do you?"

Did she? They weren't having the right

argument. Hoping to get back on track, Brenda said, "You didn't have to throw Dylan out."

"I didn't throw him out. I said he could stay until he was well."

Where was Dad's memory? Had he lost it entirely? Brenda shouted, "You did not! You said he had to be out of here in two days!" She hated crying, but she couldn't help herself. Everybody was against her. "How do you think that made him feel? That was Brandon on the phone just now. He told me that last night Dylan slept on a couch in a cabana at the beach club."

Mr. Walsh took Brenda into his arms, and she let him. He was solid and safe even if he was all wrong. While she cried into his shoulder, he said, "It's okay, Brenda. Really. It's okay. We'll all help him."

She pulled back so she could see him. While she wiped tears off her face, she said, "We will?" Had she won the argument after all?

"Brenda, try to understand. Wait, I'll show you." He opened a drawer. In it were tools, bits of wire and string, anything that didn't seem to have a place of its own. Mr. Walsh moved things around until he found something way in the back. He brought it up and cradled it in his hands.

Brenda was very surprised. She hadn't seen the thing for many years, and frankly was surprised first, that it was still in the house, and second, that her dad knew where it was.

The thing in Mr. Walsh's hands was a crude slab of glazed clay, about the size and shape of a pancake. Set into it were the prints of two tiny hands. Under the hands, the words "Brenda Walsh—Age 5" were scratched into the slab.

"Daddy, I—"

"Wait. It's important that I tell you this: Somewhere in the back of my mind, in a place I can't reach with logic or even the evidence of my eyes, you're still the little girl who made these handprints. It doesn't matter that you're in love and in high school and have the body and problems of a young woman. You're still 'Brenda Walsh—Age five.' Things happen kind of fast for us dads."

Brenda hugged her father. How could she not? He tried hard to be a no-nonsense, practical kind of guy, but she knew that beneath the granite, he was a sentimentalist full of whipped cream. Maybe that's why she was always a sucker for his smile. She said, "I guess I'm not your little girl anymore."

"Oh yes, you are. You'll always be my little girl."

He was right, and Brenda guessed it was okay. She'd have to learn to live with it. People had learned to live with more unusual situations. Kelly's friend Kyle, for one, had a lot of adjusting to look forward to.

■　■　■

Brenda and Kelly spent a lot of time moaning over the Enyart's dessert cart and saying they shouldn't, and feeling guilty about all the calories even before they'd been eaten. Brenda couldn't make up her mind between the cheesecake and the kiwi tart, but when Kelly said, "I'll have the chocolate mousse cake. Yes, definitely," Brenda ordered it, too.

The cake was thick and dreamy and so explosively chocolate, Brenda forgot for a moment about Kyle Conners. Coffee was an absolute necessity.

After they'd each had a few astonishing forks full of the cake, Brenda said, "What happened?"

Kelly looked at Brenda blankly.

"Kyle Conners, remember?"

"Right. This chocolate is awesome, isn't it?"

"Awesome chocolate. Kyle Conners?"

"He left me alone for the rest of the day, which was just as well considering the mood I was in. I would have incinerated him with a glance. But the day after, I'd recovered a little and I actually allowed Kyle to talk to me."

"What did he say?"

"He said he thought I was really beautiful, but he didn't know if I was his type. He didn't know what his type was."

"Maybe he had been thinking about his old girlfriend."

"That's what Kyle said. And I kind of bought it, you know, because he seemed so sincere and harmless. So when he asked me to join the volleyball game he was getting together, I agreed."

"He wanted to show off his pupil."

"Yeah yeah, sure sure. So we played, and the action was intense. Steve was in the game, too, and he kept punching the ball at me. Not just over the net, but at me."

"What a jerk."

"He's a jerk but he can't help it if he's in love with me. Anyway, he punched the ball and it hit me hard in the arm."

Kelly allowed Brenda to inspect her bruise. It was still an angry red thing, which Brenda found amazing considering that Kelly said it had faded a lot already.

"Anyway, when Steve did this, Kyle couldn't stand it, and he decked Steve with one punch—fighting for my honor."

"Which is more than *you* ever did," Brenda said with a leer.

"What?"

"Sorry. It's all those Marx Brothers movies Dylan took me to see. So, Kyle defended your honor."

"Yeah. And I ended up defending his, too. Because before Steve stomped away, he accused Kyle of taking an easy shot at him, and of not even being able to make it with me."

"So you said . . ." Brenda took more cake.

"So I told him that Kyle had been great in every way Steve could possibly imagine. Well, there was nothing Steve-o could say to that, so he left. I don't know where he went, but I saw him a few times later that day, and each time he asked me what had really happened between me and Kyle. I just smiled."

Kelly said nothing for a while. She ate tiny bits of cake and took tiny sips of coffee.

"That can't be all," Brenda said. "There must be a bottom line here somewhere."

"Yeah, well, there is. But before I tell you, you must swear absolutely and forever that you will never divulge what I am about to tell you."

Wondering if she would regret it later, Brenda said, "I promise."

"I hope so, Brenda, because if you ever tell, I will personally inform everybody at school that you wear pajamas with feet."

"It's not true!"

"True or not, you have nothing to worry about if you keep this to yourself. Kyle told me that he thinks he's gay."

"No." Brenda should have guessed. She was fascinated.

"Yes."

"He must really trust you if he told you that."

"He must." Kelly looked pleased with herself. She smushed the last few crumbs of cake with her fork and licked them off. She said, "You see, when we had that date on the beach, he was just testing himself. He figured if he could resist me, maybe he really was gay."

"That sounds logical."

"So, he wasn't really turning me down."

"Uh huh." Somehow, Kelly had turned this guy's identity crisis into a personal triumph. "So, are you guys going to be friends, or what?"

"Really friends," Kelly said.

Then she sighed and Brenda said, "What?"

"I was just thinking it's too bad he doesn't like girls. Kyle Conners is really quite a hunk."

Mr. Walsh promised Brenda that he would talk to Brandon, get him to try to get Dylan to come back.

"Dylan can be really stubborn," Brenda said.

Mr. Walsh smiled and reminded her that he could be pretty stubborn himself.

Kelly had worked things out with Kyle, and Brenda felt close to working things out with Dylan and her father, at least the living arrangements. With all her nerves tingling, she wanted to go to the beach club. But she could not bring herself to ditch school, not even summer school. Besides, Juliet had not yet worked things out with Romeo and this was the day for it. Brenda didn't want to miss Donna and David's performance.

Donna and David were not visible when Brenda arrived in class, but the curtain across the small stage was closed. Banging and giggling came from behind it, certainly the sound of Donna and David preparing for their giant premiere.

Mr. Suiter was sitting in the middle of the front row with his arms crossed. "Anybody alive back there?" he called.

From behind the curtain, Donna called, "We're ready."

Andrea pulled the cord that opened the curtain and revealed a scene Brenda had not expected. Everybody laughed.

David stood on a desk wearing a long velveteen dress, with something stuffed into his front to give him a bosom. He wore a frowzy blond wig and a wide hat with a long feather stuck into the band. Before him, posing with one hand upraised as if holding a glass of water on the palm, was Donna in tights and a jerkin. She looked surprisingly cute. Would the medieval look catch on?

Speaking in a falsetto, David gestured broadly as he spoke Juliet's lines:

O Romeo, Romeo! Wherefore art thou, Romeo?
Deny thy father and refuse thy name;

Or, if thou wilt not, be but sworn my love,
And I'll no longer be a Capulet.

Brenda could not stop laughing. Mr. Suiter covered his face with one hand and peeked out between the fingers.

Donna spoke in the deepest voice of which she was capable, giving the effect of a vocalizing foghorn:

Shall I hear more, or shall I speak at this?
'Tis but thy name that is my enemy;
What's in a name? that which we call a rose
By any other name would smell as sweet.

Juliet, surely the most masculine Juliet on record, said, "'Call me but love, and I'll be new baptized; Henceforth, I never will be Romeo.'"

This was dreadful. This was wonderful. Brenda couldn't make up her mind.

Evidently, Mr. Suiter couldn't make up his mind either. He thought the production was very funny, but he demanded that in a few days they do the scene again, this time seriously and with the proper casting.

Brenda wondered if Dylan would be back by then. And if he was, would she handle the situation any better this time?

When she got home from school, Dylan's Porsche was parked in front of the house. She ran up the lawn, opened the front door, and found her mom was waiting in the foyer.

"Dylan's here?" Brenda asked.

Mrs. Walsh nodded. "He's in the living room talking to your father."

Amazed, Brenda asked, "Talking? Like a conversation?"

"So far. They've been in there half an hour."

"Is he staying?"

"I don't know. Let's take it one meal at a time." She hugged Brenda and went back to the kitchen. Brenda tiptoed to the doorway between the foyer and the living room, and settled behind a bend of wall where neither her father nor Dylan could see her. She was delighted to hear that the two men sounded very chummy.

Mr. Walsh said, "Do you have any assets of your own?"

"My car. Not much else."

"Cash?"

"Zip."

A little impatiently, Mr. Walsh said, "There must be some provisions for your support."

There was a long pause. Brenda thought that Dylan must be looking at the floor, trying to decide what to say.

Dylan said, "Support, yeah. I guess everybody knows by now that I'm supposed to go to Hawaii and live with my mother."

"Not such a bad deal."

"You don't understand. In October it'll be three years since I've even seen her."

"It's true, I don't understand what's going on between you and your mother, but I know a desperate situation when I see one. Listen, Dylan: I can help you manage your finances if you let me, but you have to let me do it soon. If you put this off, first, you will be flat broke, and second, you will be in a lot of pain. And if you wait too long, the courts will step in and give you difficulties you can't even imagine." Mr. Walsh spoke as if he were advising one of his clients.

Dylan said, "I'm not sure what to do."

"I understand. This stuff doesn't get any easier as you get older." Mr. Walsh coughed in a way that Brenda believed was full of embarrassment. "Er, you can stay here for a while longer, till you sort things out."

Good old Dad, Brenda thought.

"I appreciate that," Dylan said. "And I'm sorry about the other day."

No, Dylan. Don't bring that up. Not now, while we're winning.

Brenda was relieved when her father said, "I'm the one who should be apologizing. It's hard to learn to share your daughter with another man."

Evidently, Dylan had shrugged or something. There was another long silence.

Mr. Walsh asked, "Have you talked to your father about your financial problems, about your accident?"

"No."

"Do you plan to?"

"No."

"Dylan, your dad's made a lot of mistakes, and it looks as if he's going to have plenty of time to think about them. He needs his family right now. Write him a letter. Call him. Let him know he's not alone."

"What would I say?"

"Be honest. It's not always easy, but in the long run, honesty is generally the best thing."

"The long run, yeah. I guess that's all we have left."

The silence in the living room went on and on. At last, Brenda could stand it no longer. She put on a smile and walked into the room. "Hi, guys."

That broke the mood, and soon they were talking about other things. When Mr. Walsh went into the kitchen to see if he could help his wife with dinner, Dylan and Brenda stood around awkwardly, as if they were meeting for the first time.

"Looks like you're staying," Brenda said.

"I guess. We should probably work some stuff out."

"Stuff?" asked Brenda.

"You know, like shower schedules. And I could use a little drawer space."

Dylan didn't make demands, exactly. Everything he said made sense if he was going to stay any length of time. But how long was he staying, exactly? He and Brenda were still officially not a couple, yet the longer he stayed, the greater were the chances that Mr. Walsh would find her in Dylan's arms again. How long could she be strong? How long did she want to be strong?

Steve Sanders wouldn't leave Brandon alone about playing cards in the beach club game room one night after closing. This had been going on ever since Steve ran into a guy named Danny Waterman. Evidently, Danny fancied himself some kind of cardsharp. He hadn't met Danny, but Brandon expected him to wear a broad black hat, a string tie, and a fancy silk vest.

Now, Steve was on Brandon again. Or rather on a laundry cart full of dirty towels that Brandon was pushing.

Brandon said, "I keep telling you, Steve, I'm not coming. I work too hard for my money to lose it at poker."

"But that's why you have to come, dude! You're the designated loser!"

"A guy likes to feel useful, Steve-o, but despite the honor of the thing, I'd rather not." He yelled, "Toxic waste coming through," and gave the cart a good shove. It gathered speed as it rolled down an incline. Steve leaped off just before the two laundry guys at the bottom caught it and hefted the cart into the Sea Shell Laundry Service van.

"Besides, Brandon, you're the one with the key to the game room."

"Oh, that's good. Not only will I lose all the money I already have, but I won't be able to make any more because I've been fired."

"Hey, relax. No one will ever find out. I guarantee it."

"How?"

"I don't know how, Brandon. We'll be careful. Just be there tonight, one hour after closing. And bring your keys." Steve looked both ways and skulked off between two potted palms.

Brandon wondered why he even listened to that guy.

Brenda was tired of watching Dylan mope around the house. Men who tried to be strong when they felt like garbage inside were noble, but finally wearying to be with. You always felt obligated to *notice* how noble they were being. She wished Dylan would admit how terrible he felt about being broke and then get on with his life. Maybe even visit his mom in Hawaii. Brenda had difficulty believing that going to Hawaii for *any* reason could be so bad.

Therefore, after a hard day of noticing and then *not* noticing, when Donna arrived shortly after dinner, Brenda was ready for a little recreation. Kelly had gone to Newport Beach with her mom, so deciding on a movie would be that much easier. Generally, the three of them ended up arguing on a corner in Westwood until it was too late to see any movie at all.

"We could argue here," Donna said.

"Sure. At least we could argue sitting down."

"Right." Donna glanced up the stairs and asked, "Is Dylan coming?"

"Why would he do that?"

"It doesn't have to be a date, Brenda. More of a group kind of thing, you know? Or *I* could be Dylan's date."

Oh, great, Brenda thought. First, Dylan comes to live in my house, and now, Donna offers to be my proxy date. Where would the insanity end?

Donna gauged Brenda's mood and said uneasily, "If that'll make it any easier."

Of course, going to the movies with Dylan without actually being *with him* in a date sense might be okay. She called up the stairs, "Dylan, do you want to go to the movies with Donna and me?"

Dylan surprised her by coming out of the kitchen. "No, thanks," he said as he dried his hands on a towel. "I have some reading to do."

"Come on, Dylan. It'll be our treat," Donna said.

Wrongo. Brenda could think of few things Donna might have said that would force Dylan farther back into his nobility.

"Maybe another time," Dylan said, and went upstairs.

"What's with him?" Donna asked.

"You don't want to know," Brenda said. "Let's blow this popsicle stand."

The sun balanced on the horizon and Brandon was glad that another day at the palatial Beverly Hills Beach Club was coming to an end. The day had been no more difficult than most, filled as it had been with dirty glasses, toxic towels, misplaced deck chairs, and even a diaper giving off a reek that made Brandon wrinkle his nose, even in memory.

Brandon and Henry traded quips and then Henry went home, leaving Brandon to wait for one last guy to come out of the locker room. When the guy was gone, Brandon locked up and went to sit on the steps in the lobby.

Soon it was dark, but Brandon didn't turn on any lights. Under the circumstances, he felt safer in the dark. In his mind, Brandon ran through what might happen that evening. He would lose all his money and his parents, disgusted by his flagrant contempt for the laws of chance, would disown him. He would end up on—what had Dylan called the place?—Skid Drive.

Brandon's morbid enjoyment of this romantic fantasy was interrupted by a knock at the patio door. He jumped, chuckled at his own fears, went to the door, and whispered through it, "What's the password?"

Steve's normal voice came through from the outside. "If you don't open the door right now, Walsh, I'll break your face."

"Good password," Brandon said, and opened the door, allowing three guys to enter carrying chips (potato and poker), six-packs of soda, and decks of cards. Brandon knew David Silver and wondered how he'd managed to wangle an invitation to this party. Steve considered David to be a geek, and even Brandon had a hard time with him occasionally. Steve introduced the other guy, the famous Danny Waterman.

Danny was not quite the dude Brandon had expected, but he had a lot of gel on his hair and a propensity for sneering like Elvis.

While he gawked, David exclaimed, "Wow, I've never been here at night. This is so rad."

"Can you keep it down, David?" Brandon said. "The walls have, I don't know, like, ears."

Steve threw a bag of potato chips on the table where, to Brandon, it sounded like a tiger falling into a gravel pit. He said, "Chill out, Brandon. We're here to have fun, remember?"

While Steve and Danny commandeered a green baize table and set it up to their satisfaction, David marveled at the club's electronic equipment. "This is an excellent monitor."

Steve glanced over his shoulder and said, "I like the rear-projection monitors better. That's what we have at home. Fifty diagonal inches of pure viewing pleasure."

"Yeah," said David, "but this sucker is twice as bright."

Danny sat down and began to shuffle the cards against the table. He said, "Did you ladies come to play cards or to talk?"

But David refused to be seduced away from his first love, not even to get Steve's approval. He began to mess with the CD player. "This is a very hot sound system. Why don't they ever crank it up?"

"Don't turn it on, David," Brandon said. All they needed was Motley Crue rising from the beach club in the middle of the night.

"I just want to hear one song," David said as he searched the rack.

"Just keep it down."

Danny was now doing a magician's waterfall shuffle. He smiled sweetly and asked Brandon if he was ready to lose some money.

Brandon briefly regarded Steve and thought for the millionth time that he should not be here. None of them should be here.

Brandon was surprised to find that once they began, he actually did have fun. He got into the rhythm of the game.

Danny was even more sarcastic than Steve, but Brandon just let stuff like that slide off him. Once, when Brandon looked at the mess he'd been dealt and said, "I bet a dime," Danny made fun of him, and Brandon took back the dime and bet a nickel. It obviously upset Danny that he was playing with such penny-ante guys, but Brandon thought the experience was probably good for him.

David squinted and twisted his mouth around. He claimed that he was practicing his poker face. Brandon couldn't tell if he was serious, or putting them on. Maybe David wasn't such a geek.

Steve once again told the story of how he'd won fifty bucks playing poker with Ricardo Montalban. It might even have been true. Steve's mom had been a TV mom on *Hartly House* and when he was a kid, Steve got to pal around with a lot of famous people.

They played for a few hours and Brandon began to feel the day just past as a lead cocoon that seemed to surround his body. He looked at his watch and saw he had to be back at the club in six hours. Even if Steve drove him home, he'd still have to take the bus the next morning. He'd get about four hours of sleep. He was young. He could handle it. But it wouldn't be pleasant.

By the time the evening was over, Brandon was surprised to find that he was actually about six bucks ahead.

While Brandon counted his winnings, Danny shook his head and said, "You should have been here two, three years ago when he held our traditional Ross Wienerblatt All-Night Poker Club and Chamber Music Society."

"Who's Ross Wienerblatt?" Brandon asked, though he wasn't certain he wanted to know.

Danny lowered his voice and spoke in a mysterious tone. He said, "No one knows."

It's a joke, Brandon thought, a new kind of shaggy dog story.

"They have chamber music?" David asked.

"No chamber music," Danny said. "Nobody knows why the game is called that. But the Ross Wienerblatt All-Night Poker Club and Chamber Music Society has been going on for twenty years. Once every summer, always in the middle of the night, everybody dresses like high rollers from *Guys and Dolls* or Las Vegas or something." He looked at each of them and said very seriously, "You must show you respect the game of poker. Anyway, we'd have cigars and Frank Sinatra music and babes."

"Babes?" Steve asked excitedly.

"Yeah. Great-looking babes dressed to kill, standing around just for luck."

Steve and David seemed excited by the prospect of such a party, and Brandon had to admit that he himself was fascinated. The dressing up, the music, the babes. It sounded like fun.

"Of course," Danny said offhandedly, "the main thing about a Ross Wienerblatt night is that you play for real stakes, not this penny-ante stuff." He stood up, stretched, and said, "If you guys ever want to play an adult game, give me a call. Hang loose, now."

"Uh, you hang loose, too," David called after him.

"The Ross Wienerblatt All-Night Poker Club and Chamber Music Society," Steve said, relishing the sound of it.

"Yeah," said Brandon. This could be fun.

9

The Wienerblatt

BRANDON DOZED AS STEVE DROVE HIM home. He crept into the house and then up to his room. His parents had rigged a second bed in his room so both he and Dylan could sleep in a bed instead of one of them having to sleep on the couch. The room was crowded, but Brandon could live with it. After all, Dylan was one of his best friends.

As quiet as he was, he disturbed Dylan, who claimed he'd been lying in the dark thinking about Hawaii. Brandon knew that was code. Dylan had been thinking about visiting his mother, about making peace at last, and perhaps about living on his own instead of sponging off the Walshes.

As Brandon got ready for bed, Dylan lay down and spoke to the ceiling. "You're home late."

"Yeah. I was playing poker at the club. It was awesome."

"What kind of stakes you play for?"

"Well, stakes don't matter. We were just four guys spending some time together."

Dylan sat up and turned on the light. He squinted against it and said, "Penny-ante stuff, huh?"

Brandon shrugged.

"Then you guys weren't really gambling. For a real gambler, there's no thrill unless he has a chance of going home wearing a barrel. Even so, a real gambler doesn't care about winning or losing. All he cares about is *the game*. When the question is still open, when anything can happen, that's when the rush comes for a real gambler. Which is why I don't gamble."

"Too much excitement?"

"Too much like a physical addiction. With my history, why take a chance?"

Brandon knew that Dylan had had some trouble with alcohol. Did that automatically mean he would have trouble with gambling? Who knew? Brandon said, "Fair enough."

In the bathroom, Brandon discovered that

somebody had used all the shampoo. Brenda used different stuff, something with a fancy French name and a flowery smell, so the culprit had to be Dylan. Sometimes even best bros could go too far. Maybe Brenda was right when she said that life with Dylan in the Walsh house would be just too difficult.

As he washed and got into bed, Brandon thought about the fact that he himself had had a little trouble with alcohol. Did that mean he shouldn't even consider the Ross Wienerblatt poker game? That seemed like the coward's way out. At least, that's what Steve would say. On the other hand, did it make sense for Brandon to play just because he knew he didn't have to? He fell asleep before he'd puzzled the whole thing out.

It seemed to Brandon that he fell asleep and the alarm went off simultaneously. His entire body was filled with cotton. His life was not made any easier when Dylan turned over and started to snore.

The freshness of the new day made Brandon feel a little better, and the heaviness inside him lifted as the express bus took him to the beach. He was folding towels at one end of the locker room when Henry came in looking worried. When Brandon said, "Good morning," Henry said, "You see anybody around here last night?"

"Anybody like who?" This can't be happening, Brandon thought. He tried to stay calm. Maybe Henry was talking about something else.

Henry began to fold towels, too. "Aw, it must be some of the members' kids. Most of them are okay, but every year a few of them like to sneak into the club and play cards in the middle of the night."

"How do you know?"

"I found poker chips on the floor of the game room. And a potato chip was ground into the carpet."

Who is this guy, Columbo? "Sounds pretty harmless," Brandon said encouragingly.

"Sure. Until somebody gets hurt stumbling around in the dark. Then we got police, we got insurance investigators, we got all kinds of noise, and guess whose fault it is for not locking up properly?"

"Hmm," said Brandon. Ross Wienerblatt All-Night Poker Club and Chamber Music Society or no, Brandon couldn't do this to Henry. Besides, Danny Waterman was probably a poker hustler. He'd *allowed* him to win that six bucks so Brandon would come back and lose sixty. Or six hundred.

As he left the locker room, Henry grumbled, "Just bugs me when rich kids think they own the world."

It bugged Brandon, too. Though he wouldn't

rat on his buddies, he wouldn't play their silly game either. But he had a difficult time convincing Steve of that. Brandon was sweeping leaves out of the patio when Steve sidled up to him and whispered, "Wienerblatt tonight. Midnight. Pass it on."

"What's the password?" Brandon asked.

"Password?"

"Yeah, so we'll know not to let Henry in if he shows up."

"Why should Henry show up?" Steve was bewildered. He followed as Brandon kept sweeping.

"He found out about the poker game."

"Does he know it was us?"

"No, but—"

"But nothing, Brandon. As long as he doesn't know, were still there."

"Forget it."

"You could pick up some car cash."

"No."

"Cigars."

"No."

Steve came around in front of Brandon and stopped his broom with a foot. "Babes," Steve said.

"Which ones?" Brandon shook his head to clear it. "What am I saying? I'm saying *no*!"

"You can clean up after us."

"Getting caught is not the point, Steve."

"Of course it is."

"No, it's not. The point is that Henry takes his job very seriously, and I don't like the idea of walking all over him."

"You're not walking. I am. I'll let everybody in."

This was crazy. Brandon had already made up his mind. He'd make his money the old-fashioned way—he'd earn it. And losing was a real possibility. And lying to Henry was never easy.

"Come on, Walsh."

Brandon pulled the broom out from under Steve's foot and swept away from him as hard as he could go.

Steve called, "I knew it, Walsh! I knew we could count on you! Yes!"

Brandon just kept sweeping. He ignored Steve's call to adventure.

Donna and Brenda arrived at the beach and set up their guy-watching station. Blanket arranged just so, aimed at the volleyball courts, sunblock tanning lotion, towels, sunglasses, radio, books, all within easy reach. The kitchen timer would make sure they tanned evenly without burning.

Brenda was lying on her tummy reading *A Midsummer Night's Dream* for drama class.

Sometimes it was funny, but more often, Brenda found the words impenetrable. She looked up and saw a real stud spike a volleyball at another stud on the other side of the net. Ah, summer. Ah, volleyball. What would Shakespeare say?

"Hey, Bren?" Donna said.

"Hmm?"

"What's it like living with Dylan?"

Brenda shot her a look. Donna seemed innocent, but she *always* seemed innocent. "I don't live with Dylan," Brenda said. "Not exactly. At the moment, we just happen to inhabit the same house."

"But that's what I mean." Donna set down her *Cosmo* and began to wax poetic about what she imagined the living arrangements to be. "Having him there all the time. Looking at him across the breakfast table."

"Oh, please, Donna. It's not like that at all."

"Passing him in the hall. Surprising him in the shower."

"Donna!" Brenda was genuinely shocked.

"By accident, of course," Donna assured her.

Brenda's friends obviously had minds like cesspools. Maybe this was as good a time as any to stop rumors before they grew any larger. If she told Donna something, Kelly was sure to hear it soon, and from there, word would spread to their entire set.

Brenda composed her story in her mind and said, "The truth is, Donna, Dylan and I barely talk to each other anymore."

"Yah, sure."

"Really. He just mopes in his room all day. He's always polite to my parents, but he barely talks to me or Brandon." This was so difficult. Donna was right, of course. No matter how much Dylan moped, he was still there and Brenda still loved him. Being at home was torture. If Dylan actually spoke to her, she would only feel worse because he seemed so unhappy.

"Really," Donna commented, amazed.

"Really. But the really bad part is that I don't know how to help him. It's like Dylan's father is not the only one in jail." Brenda didn't want to talk about this anymore. Actually, she never wanted to start. She turned over on her side and said no more.

She must have fallen asleep because the next thing she knew, Donna was waking her up and telling her, "Brenda, you look like a lobster."

It was true. She was sunburned so bad that on the ride home, Brenda had to sit sideways because allowing the seat to touch her back was agony.

When Brenda got home, her mom threatened her with an old family sunburn remedy, pink glop that Brenda abhorred. When Dylan saw her, he said, "Wow, Brenda, you really got a lot of color."

She loved him, but she could have done without the smart remarks. Mrs. Walsh marched her upstairs to apply the pink glop. Brenda tried to be brave. Maybe the stuff would actually do some good.

Brandon studied the contents of his closet, hoping to find something appropriate for the Wienerblatt. His knowledge of gamblers' dressing habits was based entirely on what he'd seen in movies and on TV.

James Bond always wore a tuxedo. The guys in *Guys and Dolls* wore extreme forties suits with loud patterns. Sometimes, a dress shirt open to the navel and hundreds of gold chains around the neck seemed to be the dress code.

Brandon had always admired Bond, but renting a tux was out of the question. The other styles seemed a little bizarre for the gig. At last, Brandon decided to go for a classic Murder, Incorporated, look. He had a dark suit, a black shirt, and a white tie. In the back of the closet, he dug up a set of clip on suspenders. Too bad he didn't own a pair of saddle shoes.

While Brandon was admiring his selection, Dylan came in, a little irritated.

"Hey, Dylan."

"What a day I'm having," Dylan said. "First

Brenda gets angry because I comment on her sunburn. Then your dad won't stop hassling me about calling my mom. And now, here you are preparing to wear a tie. I don't know if I can take any more excitement."

"I can't speak for Brenda or Dad, but the tie is for that poker thing tonight."

"Thanks for inviting me."

"Aren't you the one who has a problem with high rollers?"

Dylan shook his head. "I don't know what would happen to me if you Walshes weren't always looking out for my welfare." He threw himself onto his bed and ostentatiously began to read.

Brandon didn't understand what was going on, but it was obvious that Dylan was upset. He'd been upset when he walked in, so maybe the poker game was just the latest in a series of insults. Brandon said, "Look, if you want to come, then come."

"Forget it, Brandon. I got stuff to do here."

Brandon studied Dylan for a moment, but Dylan was glaring at his novel. Brandon didn't believe for a moment that Dylan was actually reading.

Brandon got dressed slowly to give Dylan a chance to talk to him. But the silence was deadly, broken only by the application of clothing to Brandon's bod, and the turning of pages by

Dylan. When he was done, Brandon took a last look at Dylan and said, "Have a nice evening."

Dylan only grunted.

Amazing. Dylan calling Brenda stubborn was really a teapot-calling-the-kettle-black situation.

Donna drove Brandon and Brenda to the beach club. The girls really looked incredible in their thrift-shop specials—long dresses, platform heels, hair piled up under tiny hats featuring long narrow feathers. Donna was even wearing a fur piece over one shoulder. When Donna saw Brandon, she said he looked like a gangster, and seemed delighted by it.

At the club, they met David Silver and Danny Waterman. David wore the loudest sport coat Brandon had ever seen. It was covered with dice and roulette wheels and cards, all worked out in sequins. The basic coat was a violent magenta. Danny was dressed more on the order of Brandon. He'd gone the extra distance and added an old brown fedora. He looked like a movie detective.

"Where's Steve?" Donna asked.

"Hiding in the showers," Brandon said. "He said he'd open the game room at exactly midnight."

"It's about that now," Brenda said.

Seconds later, meowing came from behind the door. David Silver barked.

"Don't be such a child," Donna said as the door opened.

Steve looked out at them and said with disgust, "Is that you, Silver?"

David smiled and shrugged.

Steve's outfit looked as if it had belonged to his grandfather. It was a gray double-breasted number with a lighter gray pinstripe. He actually wore saddle shoes. And somewhere, he'd found a fake mustache.

They all agreed that they looked rad and chic.

"Is this it?" Brandon asked.

"It what?" Steve said.

"You said there'd be babes here."

"What are we, Brandon?" Donna said. She put one hand on her hip and swung the tail of her dead fox with her other hand.

"Yeah," said Brenda. "I didn't put clothes on over my sunburn just to come down here and be insulted."

Brandon knew he was in trouble, but it was only because they didn't understand. "Of course, both of you are babes. Great babes. But I already know Donna, and Brenda is my sister, so she doesn't count. I thought you meant *new* babes."

Sarcastically, Steve said, "We can stand out

here and argue about it, Walsh, or we can go inside and play a little poker."

No point, Brandon decided. They all went inside.

Steve had been busy, as he took pains to remind them. Six chairs stood around the green baize table. At each place was a bowl of corn chips, a cigar like a furled umbrella, and an ashtray. To one side stood a tray full of poker chips. Steve tapped on the CD player and Frank Sinatra began to croon softly.

"I have to admit, Sanders, you're a class act."

"You got that right."

"I see you put out six chairs, Sanders," Danny said.

"Sure. One ass per seat."

"The way this is usually done," Danny said patiently, "is that the girls just stand behind us for luck. They're kind of like decor. They don't actually play."

Danny obviously was used to dealing with a different class of woman. He didn't know how deep the water was around that subject. Brenda was already pursing her lips, a sure sign that she was ready to explode. Donna would follow any lead Brenda gave her.

Brenda said, "If you're afraid we might win some money, Danny, we can leave now."

"Yes," said Donna. "Any number of guys

would be pleased to be graced by the presence of a couple of babes such as ourselves."

Brandon said, "I don't think Wienerblatt would mind."

Danny looked around the table and saw that he was alone in his opinion. He shrugged and said, "Why not?"

Everybody settled down and began to play. Brandon was not the only one to have trouble smoking a cigar, but for the sake of the Wienerblatt tradition, all of them but David continued to take an occasional puff.

Danny stopped dealing and said, "Ain't you going to light yours, Silver?"

"Are you kidding? It might stunt my growth."

"Too late," Steve said around his own cigar, and everybody laughed.

Brandon held up his cigar and announced, "Mmm. Zesty and minty fresh." He coughed and asked Steve, "Where did you get these El Ropeo numbers?"

"These happen to be very fine cigars."

"Cuban?" Donna asked.

"Probably more like they're from San Bernardino," Danny said. "Are we playing cards, or what?" He began dealing again.

"Deal me in."

The voice came from the door, and everybody turned toward it, startled. Standing by the door looking very serious, was Dylan. He wasn't dressed for the Wienerblatt, but he was definitely ready to play poker.

After hearing Dylan's comments about gambling, Brandon was surprised to see him here. He said, "You sure about this, man?"

Dylan said, "I'm sure." He walked into the light cast by the single overhead lamp and threw a wad of bills onto the table. "Deal me in."

"Deal the man in," said Steve.

Dylan pulled around another chair and sat down. Brandon could see that Brenda was not happy. She was wrecking herself trying to avoid Dylan, but life kept flinging him into her face. Actually, Dylan's presence changed the tone of the game for all of them. They'd been having a wild time playing for real stakes, pretending they were high rollers from Vegas, smoking cigars, talking tough. But now, they had caught Dylan's attitude, and the laughter evaporated. This was no longer a game, but grim business.

Brandon couldn't help wondering where Dylan's money came from, and where Dylan would get more if he lost. Chances were good that Dylan's thoughts were along the same lines.

They played a few hands and money moved around the table quite a bit. Dylan had the perfect poker face. Under normal circumstances, it was difficult to know what he was thinking. Now, when he was trying not to betray the quality of his hand, knowing his thoughts was impossible.

They played a hand during which each of them dropped out, one by one, until the only players left in the game were Dylan and David. Brandon found it amazing that the coolest guy in school was up against some geek. But *cool* didn't matter here. Only the cards mattered.

A long time passed after Dylan raised David fifty bucks. David squirmed in his chair.

Steve said, "Come on, David."

"How much to stay in?"

"Seventy-five big ones." Danny sounded as if he was enjoying David's discomfort.

David threw seventy-five dollars' worth of chips into the pot. Everyone nodded. Brandon admired David's bravery. Dylan had not bluffed all evening. When he played as if he had the big cards, he had the big cards. Dylan stood on the cards he had.

"Big Dave?" Danny asked.

David studied his cards, wide eyed. "Two. No, three. No, two. Four."

Brenda and Donna rolled their eyes. Steve said, "Come on, Silver."

"Three. Definitely three." He threw down three cards and Danny dealt him three replacements.

Dylan bet another fifty and David covered him.

Dylan looked at Brandon and asked, "Will you stake me fifty?"

"Sorry, man. I'm running on fumes."

"How about you, Sanders? My credit good?"

Steve looked uncomfortable, but he said, "Sure." He threw in a fifty-dollar bill.

Danny said, "The pot stands at four hundred dollars."

Brandon could hear breathing. Cigar smoke rose into the air like gray spider webs. Sinatra sang softly about doing it his way.

"So," said Dylan, "what you got?"

David turned over his cards. "One ace, and four twos."

Dylan slammed down his cards and shook his head. "I don't believe it. I take a dive with a full boat."

Brandon could see Dylan was in pain. That wasn't just money on the table, it was his life. After the flush of victory, David looked horror-stricken, and Brandon guessed he would have given the money back if anyone had suggested it. But no one suggested it. They knew, as Brandon did, that Dylan would not have taken the money anyway, and the gesture would only have made him feel worse.

Dylan stood up and said, "Thanks for the buggy ride, ladies and gentlemen. It's been vivid." He walked toward the door and Brandon leaped up to follow him.

At the doorway, Brandon whispered, "You okay, man?"

Dylan didn't look at Brandon when he said, "I'm fine, just a little wound up. Probably take a ride up the coast. You keep playing. Have a good time."

"I'm really sorry."

"Forget it, Brandon. The Walshes aren't responsible for the way I live my life despite what they may believe."

And then he was gone, leaving Brandon wounded by Dylan's accusation. Was it possible to help somebody too much?

Thoughtfully, he walked back to the table and sat down. While Brandon had been at the door, somebody had gathered up the cards and now they sat in a deck before Steve. He picked them up and riffled them. "Shall I deal?"

But the thrill was gone. Nobody felt like playing. For all of them, Brandon said, "I feel kind of weird now. Let's just call it a wrap."

Steve kept his promise and allowed Brandon to clean up. He carried the chairs back where they belonged, checked the floor for potato chips, and made certain that Danny had all the gambling equipment. Before he left, Brandon looked one last time at the room. As far as he could tell, it was clean. He turned off the light, then followed Brenda and Donna to the parking lot.

On the drive home, Brandon mentally inspected the state in which he'd left the game room. He hoped Columbo didn't find any evidence. And where was Dylan? As depressed as he was, he might do anything. Brandon tried not to worry. Maybe Dylan was right: he'd had enough of the Walshes for a while.

The next day, the night before really wore on Brandon, but he managed to keep up a lively front for the sake of the customers and for the sake of his job. Steve came by as he was unpacking deck chairs and tried to convince Brandon he knew the Laker girls just because he'd seen them on his big-screen TV.

Henry walked over to them looking worried about something. He said, "Hey, Sanders, you have a poker game here last night?"

Brandon tried to stay casual, but inside, everything froze.

"Me?" said Steve. "Poker game? Here? Last night? Naw. I was with Brandon."

Sure, thought Brandon. Dump it all on me. He had a choice of staying true to the beach club or supporting a friend. He hated lying to Henry, but only one choice was possible. "Right, Henry. He was with me. What's the prob?"

"Come on. I'll show you." He marched off with Steve and Brandon following. They shrugged at each other. Henry wasn't angry about somebody using his game room after hours. This was a much bigger deal.

He took them into the game room and held up a hank of wires that led into the wall. The TV was gone, the stereo system, the VCR, everything!

Steve said, "Something tells me you didn't send all this stuff out to have the transistors polished."

"You got *that* right. We had a major burglary last night."

Brandon flashed on Dylan losing four hundred bucks all at a crack. Dylan wasn't used to poverty. Had he done something drastic? It was difficult to believe, but how well did any of them really know Dylan?

10

Inside job

AFTER THAT, THE EXCITEMENT NEVER stopped. Henry locked the game room and had Brandon set up a barricade of deck chairs in front of it. A few of the older club members complained, but when Brandon explained about the robbery, they all appreciated the seriousness of the situation and stood around discussing the possibilities.

The police arrived in black-and-whites. In charge of the investigation was Detective Pena, a brusque, middle-aged woman who was all business. Henry opened the game room for her and the forensic crew spread out to dust for prints and search for clues. Henry gave Detective Pena a list of what had been stolen.

Her first guess was that the robbery had been an inside job because entry had not been forced. Detective Pena's conclusions compelled Brandon to think about the Wienerblatt; he went over again the condition in which he'd left the game room. Had he locked the door? Had they closed all the windows? Before Henry had announced the robbery, Brandon had been certain that they had locked the place up tight, but now he wasn't so sure.

Henry apprehensively stood at the doorway and watched Detective Pena and her people at work.

"Take it easy, Henry," Brandon said. "Nobody's going to blame you for this."

"You don't know all the facts, Walsh. Sooner or later, they're going to dig up my old police record."

"Your what?" Brandon said with surprise.

Henry continued watching through the doorway as the police moved around the room. "I was just a little older than you. Out cruising around with my buddies. Anyway, I fell asleep in the back seat and my friends got this bright idea to rip off a house in Culver City." Henry shook his head. "To make a long story short, next thing I knew I was being charged with breaking and entering, same as the others."

"But that's not fair."

"Fair doesn't matter. The important thing right now, with all these police around, is that I wanted you to hear it from me first."

As if on cue, Detective Pena came out of the game room and asked to speak to Henry, who raised his eyebrows at Brandon and followed Detective Pena inside.

Brandon felt really bad for Henry. He was certain that none of the Wienerblatt participants had anything to do with the robbery, but Brandon could not help feeling guilty, as if their smaller trespassing crime had somehow encouraged the robbery to happen. Give it a rest, Brandon. That's all just so much sea foam. Connecting the two crimes was foolish. Still, the feeling would not go away.

Steve seemed to take a lot of pleasure from the investigation. He kept singing the *Dragnet* theme into Brandon's ear. "Dum de dum dum," he'd sing. He thought it was really strange and interesting that this kind of thing had happened on the very night they'd chosen for their Ross Wienerblatt card game.

"Yeah, interesting," Brandon said. But the fact that Steve had been entertaining himself with the same thoughts that had been worrying Brandon somehow made the truth of them seem more real.

"Dum de dum dum," Steve sang.

"I don't know what *you're* so happy about."

"Lighten up, Walsh. This robbery has nothing to do with us."

Should he tell Steve about Henry's record? Brandon decided against it. Henry's past was none of Steve's business. Brandon said, "You got me to lie to Henry."

"A little white lie." Steve held up his fingers to show how small a lie it was.

Steve's attitude made Brandon angry. He had to do something to wipe that smirk off Steve's face, and maybe make himself feel better about this whole nasty business. He said, "It wasn't little for me. And certainly not for Henry." He turned and walked toward the game room.

"Where you going, man?"

"I'm going to straighten this out right now."

"You'll lose your job."

Brandon looked back at Steve and said, "You don't care about my job. All you care about is Steve Sanders."

As Brandon entered the room, Steve called after him, "Don't blow this, Walsh."

It all depended on your definitions. Brandon wasn't going to blow anything. For a change, he was going to set things right.

Henry and Detective Pena were surprised by what Brandon had to say. The good part was that the police lost interest in Henry—for the moment, at least—and Brandon became an object of great fascination. Detective Pena asked Henry to pull the addresses and phone numbers of the other Wienerblatt players from the beach club files.

Henry said, "If what you want is to round up those kids, you don't have to do that. They're all here at the club. I've seen them."

Brandon and Henry got the kids together outside the game room, where they stood in a worried clump. The uniformed policewoman watching them wouldn't allow them to speak to each other, fearing they would concoct a story among themselves. But that didn't prevent the kids from glaring at Brandon. He knew he'd betrayed their trust, but he kept telling himself that there are more important things than keeping a private poker game a secret. He was really torn.

Detective Pena called in the kids one at a time. First, Danny Waterman, then Brenda, then Steve, then Donna, then David. She came out with David and asked to see Dylan.

Nobody else spoke, so Brandon said, "He's not here."

"Do we know where he is?" Detective Pena asked.

"No. But as soon as he comes home I'll tell him to call you."

"Thanks. Mr. Walsh?"

Brandon followed Detective Pena into the game room, and she closed the door. He told her about the Ross Wienerblatt All-Night Poker Club and Chamber Music Society. She reminded him that what they had done was trespassing at the very least, but she seemed less interested in the game itself than in the circumstances surrounding the game. Was anybody around when they arrived? Was anybody around when they left? Had they noticed any open doors or windows?

Brandon was disappointed and angry with himself that he hadn't noticed any of this stuff; he just wasn't a trained observer.

Detective Pena also seemed interested in the fact that Dylan was depressed because he'd lost a lot of money in the game, and hadn't left with everybody else.

Brandon said, "You have to understand that even if Dylan's in real money trouble, he'd never steal. He's just not like that."

"You know him well?"

"Pretty well. As well as anyone can."

Detective Pena thanked Brandon for his time and walked outside with him. She told him and the others, "Don't leave town," and went back into the game room.

Brandon asked, "So, how did it go with you guys?"

Danny Waterman said, "These pigs don't seem to understand the difference between trespassing and borrowing something your parents pay through the nose for."

"What do you expect?" Steve said. "That lady detective had never even heard of my mother. All she wanted to talk about was whether we locked up or not."

"That's important, isn't it?" Brenda asked.

"Sure, it's important. But they have a lot of nerve accusing us. I don't have to steal stereo equipment. What did she ask you?"

"She just wanted to know what had happened. I admitted that I stole a package of gum when I was seven. I was really relieved when she didn't hold that against me."

"That's my sister, the crime lord," Brandon said.

David said, "I thought she was going to really let me have it because of all the money I won, but she didn't care about that either."

Donna said, "I told her I threw up because of the cigar."

"That must have been helpful," Steve said.

"That's just what she said, that I'd been helpful."

"Frankly," Danny said, "I don't care what was helpful as long as that detective doesn't tell my parents about this. Not only will I be grounded for life, but they'll take away all my books on poker."

"Tough," Brandon said.

■　■　■

Brenda was in her room trying to compose a letter to her grandmother, but her mind kept going back to Dylan. No one had seen him since the poker game the night before, and now, because of the robbery, the police wanted to talk to him. Brandon made it sound as if Dylan was their prime suspect. Anyone who knew Dylan also knew that he could never have done such a thing. She just wished he would come back from wherever he was so that she could stop worrying about him.

At the same moment she had to go to the bathroom, she heard the shower. She sighed. Timing is everything. She padded down the hall and stopped when she saw Brandon in the middle of his room staring at the closed bathroom door.

"I guess that isn't you in the shower," Brenda said.

"No. It's Dylan."

It was important for Brenda not to show her concern. After all, she and Dylan weren't dating. Casually, she said, "Oh, he's back?"

"Yeah. He says he slept in his car up at the Ventura County line."

"He has a lot to think about," Brenda said defensively.

"Well, he's not thinking about the robbery.

When I told him what happened, he acted as if I was reporting a nit on my sweater." He picked up a knapsack on his bed. "And I wish he'd dump his stuff on his side of the room." He was about to fling the knapsack onto Dylan's bed, when he stopped and pulled an envelope from an outside pocket. "Can you beat that? He's going to Hawaii after all."

Brenda stepped into the room to get a look at the tickets. She knew that Dylan and his mom didn't get along. If he really was going to Hawaii, he must be down to last resorts. She pulled the tickets from Brandon's hand and after examining them, said, "He must have just decided to go. See? The ticket was made up today."

"How could he buy it today? He lost all his money last night."

It was a puzzle all right. And Dylan didn't have any credit cards either. Brenda didn't like the direction this conversation was going. She said, "Well, he got the money somewhere, okay? Just leave him alone."

Brandon took the tickets back from her and tapped them against his palm while he regarded the bathroom door. He spoke as if Brenda wasn't even there. "The club gets ripped off, and suddenly Dylan has money, and he's spending it to blow town. If I were the suspicious type—"

"He's not 'blowing town,' Brandon, he's just visiting his mother. I can't believe you're even thinking this! Dylan's not some sneak thief. He's our *friend*."

"That must be why he uses all my shampoo."

"This isn't about shampoo, is it, Brandon?"

For some reason, Brenda's reasonable question caused Brandon to get very angry. He stuffed the tickets back into the knapsack and said, "I'm sorry, Bren, but I've just had a really classic, outstanding day during which I found out who my friends really are. Okay?"

"Fine. End of conversation. I'm going to the bathroom."

Brenda used her mom's bathroom, and as she walked back along the hall—thank goodness Brandon's door was closed—she heard the doorbell ring. "I'll get it," she cried. The letter to Grandma wasn't going very well, anyway.

Brenda opened the door and found herself face to face with Detective Pena. "Oh," Brenda said in surprise.

"Does Dylan McKay live here?" Detective Pena asked.

"Yes."

"Is that his Porsche?"

"Yes."

"That one in your driveway with the VCR, the amplifier, and the fax machine under a blanket behind the front seat?"

"I guess. It *looks* like Dylan's car."

"I came over here to speak with young McKay. Now, I'm afraid I'll have to ask him to come down to the station for questioning."

This was terrible. Was Brenda the only person in the world who believed that Dylan was innocent? Not innocent, maybe, but honest?

11

Parting gifts

DETECTIVE PENA TOOK DYLAN TO THE
police station in her unmarked car, and the
Walshes followed in *their* unmarked car. All the
time, Mrs. Walsh went on about how awful it
was that such a fine boy as Dylan was being
treated like a criminal. Brenda knew her mom
well enough to know that she wasn't just patronizing Brenda. Mrs. Walsh really felt that way.
Brandon, on the other hand, didn't say much.

Brenda said, "He told everybody the stuff in
the car was his. Why can't anybody believe
him?"

"I'd like to believe him, Bren," Brandon said,

"but it doesn't make sense to me that he'd be driving around with all that electronic gear hidden in his car."

Brandon persisted in not understanding. "It wasn't hidden," Brenda said.

"It was under a blanket."

"He probably didn't want it to get stolen."

Brandon laughed in a way that Brenda thought was nasty and uncalled for.

"Enough," Mr. Walsh cried.

By the time they got to the police station, nobody was talking to anybody.

As far as Brenda was concerned, the high point of the entire trip was her dad's performance at the police station. They'd been sitting in the very depressing green waiting room when some man came out of an office and asked Mr. Walsh if Detective Pena was still talking to Dylan. When Dad said she was, the guy shook his head and said, "Like father, like son."

Dad stood up and said, "Has he been charged with anything?"

"No."

"Then why are you condemning him for what his father did, or *may have* done?"

Was this the same guy who hadn't wanted her to go out with Dylan because his father was a crook? Brenda was amazed and gratified. She looked across the room to where Brandon was getting a drink of water. Now, it was

Brandon who didn't trust Dylan. It was as if her
father and her brother had traded brains.

The guy from the office glared at Mr. Walsh
as if he were a slug on the sidewalk and asked,
"Are you his lawyer?"

"No. I'm just somebody who knows him.
You obviously don't."

The guy held his gaze a little longer and
walked away. "Nice talking to you," the guy said
sarcastically.

"Likewise, I'm sure," Mr. Walsh said.

When the guy was out of earshot, Mrs.
Walsh patted Brenda on the hand and said
proudly, "Well, what about your father?"

"Way to go, Dad," Brenda said.

Only Brandon seemed unimpressed.

When they got back home, Dylan returned
to the shower because he'd been interrupted by
Detective Pena. The truth was, Brandon felt pretty grungy himself and he was in no mood to wait
around to use his own bathroom. Especially
when it was being used by somebody Brandon
was sure was not being straight with him.
Brandon felt a little like an idiot, too, because
despite his current suspicions about Dylan,
Brandon had been keeping an important fact
from the police and hoping the situation would
clear up before he felt obligated to tell them.

Brandon yelled through the bathroom door, "I hope you're not using all my shampoo! Oh, wait! I forgot! You can't use all my shampoo now because you *already* used all my shampoo!"

Dylan came out of the bathroom wearing a fluffy white robe—supplied by Mrs. Walsh—and fiercely rubbing his hair with a towel. He said, "What the hell is bugging you? And don't say shampoo."

"You're right," Brandon said angrily. "It's not really *my* problem. It's between you and the police, isn't it? But don't worry. I'll never tell."

Mystified, Dylan asked, "Tell what?"

"About the pawn tickets," Brandon exclaimed. "The pawn tickets you threw away in *my* wastebasket. I could have mentioned those to the police and put you in the can for years."

"In the can for what? Pawning my own stuff?"

What colosal nerve the guy had, what Andrea Zuckerman called *chutzpah*. "Yeah, right. I know what stuff you have. It's all over my room."

Dylan shook Brandon by the shoulders and pleaded with him. "Will you stop shouting for a minute, Brandon, and listen to me?"

Brandon folded his arms and sat down on his bed. This had better be good, he thought.

"That was my stuff, but I wasn't keeping it here. It was at my family storage locker." Dylan sat

down across from Brandon on his own bed. He
balled up the towel as he spoke. "You have no idea
what it's like to go back day after day and select
the part of my life I'm going to pawn next. One
day, it's my skis. The next, it's my guitar. Or my
stereo equipment, or my grandfather's watch. Not
to mention having to deal with that really offensive
woman at the pawn shop. All just to stay afloat."

"Dylan, I—" Brandon had been an absolute
jerk.

"I didn't want to tell you this, but I put my
Porsche up for sale. It'll be the last thing to go."

Quietly, Brandon asked, "What about the
ticket to Hawaii?"

"It seemed like a good time to visit my
mom."

"The flake? The woman you haven't seen in
three years?"

"We talked on the phone for an hour. She
paid for the ticket."

Brandon felt that he might not be such a
jerk after all. Every conclusion he'd come to had
been made on the basis of the evidence. How
could he be expected to—? Brandon said, "Why
didn't you tell us?"

After a long time, Dylan took a deep breath
and said, "I couldn't. I'm not the kind of guy who
goes running home to mommy."

They sat across from each other for a while
without saying anything. Maybe it wasn't so easy

being Dylan McKay. Sure, everybody thought you were totally cool, and you could have any girl you wanted, but responsibilities went with the job. Stuff that other guys could get away with because they were just mortals would cause wild comment if done by Dylan McKay. And even if a guy like Dylan McKay didn't care what anybody else thought, he had a certain amount of self-respect to maintain. For that moment, anyway, Brandon was glad he was Brandon.

Not that the life of Brandon Walsh was necessarily a bed of roses. For the second time that summer, Brandon went to work wondering if he still had a job. The first time, Jerry Rattinger had almost gotten him fired. Now, the situation was much worse because he had done in himself. If Henry was going to fire him, it was because Brandon had lied about the poker games. Well, Brandon would take it without a blindfold.

Brandon found Henry on the deck outside his office watching "The Young and the Restless" on a portable TV. The theme music came up, Henry flicked off the TV and he turned to study Brandon. The guy was good, Brandon had to admit. He couldn't tell if Henry was angry or what.

Brandon said, "Henry, do I still work here?"

"Again, Walsh? You have the nerve to ask me that again?"

"I—"

Henry spoke as if to the ocean. "I could be royally ticked off that you lied to me, or I could be pleased that you told the police the truth. I don't know. I guess I'll be both for a while. I mean, somewhere inside the scrawny teenage body is a pretty good kid."

"Thanks, Henry."

Brandon was on his way down the stairs when Henry said, "And Walsh?"

Brandon turned and waited.

"You'll be delighted to hear that the Los Angeles Beach Club, up the road, got hit last night. Exact same kind of robbery as we had."

There must be a point here somewhere, but Brandon couldn't see it. "Great, Henry."

"Let's have a little enthusiasm, Walsh. This time they caught the guys."

"Who?"

"It was those guys from Sea Shell, the laundry service used by us and every other club on the beach! Or should I say formerly used?"

"Wow! I have to call Dylan."

"No need. I already did."

Brandon was relieved that he had not been wrong about Dylan after all. No matter how broke he got to be, Dylan was just not the type who steals.

■   ■   ■

Brenda went back to the beach, but this time she was completely covered. She wore pants, a shirt, sunblock, and a very trendy floppy hat. She was lying next to Donna, still working on her letter to Grandma, when David Silver came by and showed Donna a thick roll of bills. He asked her, "Buy you a snack, little girl?"

Donna just said, "Oh, please," and put her nose further into her *Money* magazine.

Disappointed, David put his money into a pocket and walked away.

Not long after that, Brenda got the surprise of her life when Andrea showed up. She claimed that for the first time, she was ready to get a tan. From her beach bag she pulled a clutch of newspaper clippings. "I'm going to do it right, of course."

"This is the best way," Brenda said, and rummaged through her own beach bag. She plopped another floppy hat onto Andrea's head and said, "One size fits all."

Brenda and Andrea laughed. Andrea put away her clippings and did not remove the hat all afternoon.

That evening, Dylan came into Brenda's room to say good-bye. He almost didn't hug her because he was afraid of hurting her sunburn, but Brenda assured him that she was all better. "That pink stuff of my mom's smells awful, but it really works."

They stood there for a while, breathing into each other's ears. Dylan said, "It really means a lot to me that you thought I was innocent."

"Not innocent," Brenda said playfully. "But honest."

"Yeah, right. Whatever it was, I feel good about it."

"It was easy for me. I believed you."

"You are amazing. I almost didn't believe myself. I mean, what if there was more of my father in me than I thought? After all, Brandon is a lot like his father. It's one of the things I like about him."

Brenda sensed that the mood was getting too heavy for a simple good-bye. Dylan was just going to visit his mother. And he would be back. Brenda said, "Well, you have to promise me you'll have a good time."

"Yeah, sure. And you have to promise me something, too."

"What?"

"Take it easy with the sun, will you?"

Brenda laughed and cried at the same time as they hugged. Her back really didn't hurt much.

Brandon was at his desk reading a book of Hemingway short stories. He was a hero of Brandon's. The guy had been a journalist who'd been everywhere and done everything. Of course, the suicide at the end was kind of a bummer, but Brandon felt that he could work around that.

Dylan's open suitcase was on his bed, full and ready to go. Brandon felt like a major jerk for having doubted him, and he would do everything he could to make them part as friends. He had something very specific in mind.

Dylan came in and said, "Hey, Brandon, you want to search my luggage for any of your stuff."

Brandon jumped to his feet and said, "What? Who, me?" He smiled in what he hoped was a self-deprecating way. "I hope we're past all that."

"We are," Dylan said, and they shook hands.

"And just to show you there are no hard feelings, I got a little something for you."

"You didn't have to—"

Brandon opened a desk drawer and pulled out a bottle of shampoo tied with a single red ribbon. When Dylan saw it, he laughed.

"Well, I knew you used the stuff, so I thought, you know."

"I know. I got something for you, too." Dylan reached around and pulled something from his suitcase. It was an identical bottle of shampoo.

They both laughed harder than ever.

Dylan was a great guy, and his life was shaping up; Brandon still had his job; and Brenda had survived both her drama class and her sunburn. It was a most excellent Beverly Hills kind of summer.

1

Popping up

IN THE TERRIBLE BEVERLY HILLS HEAT,
shimmering devils danced in the street, and even the
big stucco houses looked somehow unreal, like
movie sets. The sky was a hard, flat blue holding the
white-hot marble of the sun.

Brenda Walsh felt sweaty and gritty. Her clothes
stuck to her body. Wisps of long dark hair stuck to
her face. She was positive that weather during the
school year should not be like this. It certainly never
had been this way back in Minnesota, where her
family came from. One of the few advantages of living in Minneapolis as opposed to Beverly Hills was
that you would not melt while walking home from
the video store during November.

She stopped before attempting to walk up the

gentle incline of the driveway, and just stood there breathing in and out the hot soup of the atmosphere. Up near the garage her brother, Brandon, leaned far under the hood of his car. His feet kicked the air as if he were attempting to swim down into the depths of the engine. She didn't know how he could work in this weather.

Brandon called his car Mondale. It was a few years old, and worse yet, it was a boxy blue Japanese thing—hardly the car of choice even among high-school kids in Beverly Hills. Life was difficult when your parents were not rich.

Brenda struggled up the driveway and sank gratefully into the shade of a big old tree. Ineffectually, she fanned herself with one hand. More to herself than to Brandon, she said, "Where is winter, already? I need a season I can sulk and be depressed in."

Brandon wriggled out of the engine compartment and, while he tossed a screwdriver, said, "Don't tell me, Bren. You're baby-sitting tonight and all the video stores were out of *Dirty Dancing*."

"I had to go to three places before I found it." The thought frustrated her all over again, but raising her voice was too great an effort.

Brandon really looked disgusting. To start with, the T-shirt he was wearing was full of holes; it must have been the oldest one in his drawer. Then, grease had been liberally applied. Sweat stains spread under his arms and down his front. He was a fragrant mess. "You must have that movie memorized by now," he said.

"Whatever gets you through the night. Isn't that what you always say?"

The sound of metal rollers came from under the car, and Dylan McKay slid out on a mechanic's trolley. "No, that's what *I* always say," he said with a smirk.

This was terrible. Here she'd been mentally criticizing Brandon for his appearance, but after her walk to the video stores she looked almost as bad as he did. Without the grease, of course. But enough sweat was soaked into her West Beverly High T-shirt to float battleships. "Er, hi. I didn't see you."

"I saw you."

Great. Say something, dummy. But before she had a chance to open her mouth again, her mother called from the house that Brenda had a phone call. Saved by the bell.

"Excuse me," Brenda said. "Probably a very important call from the president."

As she walked into the house she lamented the fact that she was wearing her old baggy jeans instead of something a little more chic. Inside, the house was dim and cool. Her mother looked very comfortable in shorts and a cotton shirt. The sweat actually felt cold against Brenda's skin.

She dropped *Dirty Dancing* on the kitchen table and eagerly picked up the phone. At the other end was Mrs. Ross, Katie's mom. Mr. and Mrs. Ross would not need Brenda's baby-sitting services that evening. Katie had chicken pox, and the Ross family was staying home.

Brenda nodded philosophically. First Dylan saw her at her absolute worst, and now her baby-sitting job fell through. She had spent the entire afternoon hunting for *Dirty Dancing* for nothing.

If she were not to spend the evening at home playing Scrabble with her parents—a thought that made her shudder—she had to make other plans fast. There was only one thing to do. She went upstairs, and in the privacy of her room called Kelly Taylor.

Kelly was a lithe, beautiful blonde who had taken Brenda under her well-manicured wing when the Walshes had first arrived from Minnesota. As the weeks and months had gone by, Kelly had taught Brenda how the social game was played at Beverly Hills High. They were very good friends, maybe even best friends.

While the phone rang, Brenda girded herself for the unpleasant task to come. Kelly answered the phone and Brenda hesitated, then said, "All right. I'll do it. I'll go out with your dweeb cousin Algernon."

"That's okay," said Kelly. "I convinced Donna to do it."

Donna was the third member of their core set. She had some learning problems and was perhaps not as bright as Kelly or Brenda, but she was really very nice: a knockout blonde with a killer figure. Brenda was disappointed to hear that Donna had agreed to do the deed. Even going out with Algernon would have been better than nothing.

"Want to come over?" Kelly asked.

The air was hot. Brenda was disgusted. Maybe she would watch *Dirty Dancing* after all. "No," she said shortly. "I think I'll just stay home and organize my sock drawer."

"You don't sound good, Brenda. You need a bubble bath."

Sure. A bubble bath, a date with Tom Cruise, a major credit card with no limit, the list went on and on. She and Kelly talked for a while longer, but Brenda's heart wasn't in it. They hung up and Brenda sat on her bed tapping on *Dirty Dancing* and listening to somebody racing Mondale's engine.

The engine dropped into a purr and Brandon said, "Hey, Dad. Check this out. This baby is humming."

Curious, Brenda went to the window and looked down. Her dad, Brandon, and Dylan were standing around admiring Mondale. Brandon and Dylan were wiping their hands on rags that were nearly as dirty as what they were trying to clean.

Mr. Walsh peered at Dylan and said, "So, where'd you learn to work on cars?"

Dylan shrugged. He was kind of cute when he did that. "From working on cars, I guess. Same as Brandon."

"Except that Dylan has a Porsche," Brandon said.

Mr. Walsh nodded as if he understood. "Nice car," he said.

Brenda recognized the tone of voice her father was using. He didn't like Dylan and he was looking for evidence to support his feelings. When he said "nice car," what he really meant was, "too nice a car for a kid your age."

Mr. Walsh continued, pushing his way further out of bounds. "Bought it with your paper-route earnings, did you?"

Dad could be such a jerk. Brenda didn't want to listen anymore. She would have closed the window, but the breeze was nice. She wondered if there was any grape soda in the refrigerator. Actually a grape soda and a bubble bath sounded pretty good. As she walked out of her room Dylan's soft laughter faded behind her.

But when Brenda came back from the kitchen, grape soda in hand, Brandon was already in the bathroom, and steam from the shower was pouring into her room through the half-open door. "Brandon!"

The shower stopped and Brenda yelled into the bathroom, "Can't you shut the door? It's hot enough in here already—oh!"

Looking at her around the shower curtain was not Brandon but Dylan. He smiled and said, "Sorry," as Brenda backed quickly from the room and leaned the door closed, a little breathless.

She was not just embarrassed. She was excited, too. Dylan was *so* gorgeous. And here he was in her actual shower. She would never have gone so far as to plan such a thing, but she saw nothing wrong with enjoying it now that it had happened. She called through the door, "You keep popping up on me today."

"Who popped up on who?"

Brenda hugged herself. This was great. He was flirting with her.

"You like any movies besides *Dirty Dancing*?" he called out.

"Some," she said cautiously.

"Ever see *Animal Crackers*?"

"Is that a movie or a snack?"

"It's a Marx Brothers comedy. And if you've never seen it on the big screen, you're really missing something. Too bad you're working tonight."

"Actually my clients chickened out. I'm free." She labored mightily not to sound too eager.

"Great. Want to come with me and Brandon?"

Did she? Did she ever? "I'm there," she said casually. She leaped into the air, pumped one arm and mouthed a silent *yes!*

Brenda would have liked to ride in Dylan's Porsche, but Brandon insisted on giving Mondale a test drive. The guys' discussion about auto mechanics made a pleasant babble in the background while the cool evening air blew into Brenda's face through the open window.

She wondered what Dylan was really like and whether he could ever be interested in a girl like her. She knew he had a reputation for being wild and dangerous, but Brandon seemed to like him and that was usually a good sign. Actually, she could use a little wildness in her life about now. She had frightened herself badly when she had actually offered to go out with Kelly's cousin Algernon.

They arrived at the mall where the theater was and Brenda enjoyed the dry comments Dylan made about the people who walked by while they waited in line. But her fun was cut short by the approach of a young woman heading straight toward Dylan.

She was surprised by how jealous she felt. After all, she and Dylan had barely met. She certainly had no claim on him. And yet, when he spoke with the absolutely awesome blonde who seemed to know him (Brandon was frankly fascinated), Brenda took

Dylan's arm and held it till the other girl left.

Brandon continued to watch the sway of the awesome blonde as she threaded her way through the crowd. Without looking away, he casually asked, "Friend of yours?"

"Yeah, we used to hang out," Dylan said. "I'd introduce you, but I forgot her name."

"Terrific," Brenda said sarcastically.

"Not my fault," Dylan said. "She kept changing it. She was Tanya for a while. And then Rainbow. For a while she called herself Millicent. Who can blame the poor kid? I think her real name is something like Gertrude, or Beatrice, or Brenda."

Brenda was pretty sure Dylan was just kidding, but just to show she was paying attention, she punched him in the arm, hard.

Dylan gingerly rubbed the spot she'd hit and chuckled. "Mean right hook."

Brandon had been smiling for some time. He said, "Yeah. And who do you think she practices on?"

The Marx Brothers were as funny as Dylan had promised, though Brenda thought their attitude toward women needed a little adjustment. After the show Brandon drove while Dylan guided them to an exclusive complex of condos in the hills above Beverly Hills. It was a thing of beauty hidden among stone walls and dwarf palm trees.

They left Brandon's car with the man on duty and went up in the elevator to the McKay condo. Inside, it was furnished in ostentatious good taste. Glass walls looked out on what might have been primeval forest, but had probably been installed by a landscaping company. A fireplace big enough to house a family of four dominated the living room. Dylan chose a few compact discs from a library of hundreds and put one of them into the player. Music boomed from all around them. The sound quality was so good, the music did not seem to be recorded at all, but live. Dylan put the good sounds down to the quality of the sub-woofers, the hyper-tweeters, and the midrange boffers.

When Dylan went to answer the doorbell (it rang a little riff by Bach), Brenda took the opportunity to say to Brandon, "Thanks for letting me come with you guys."

"If you play your cards right, we might do it again." He winked at her. Dylan walked back into the room carrying a big cardboard box that brought with it the odors of hot grease and grilled meat. "What do you say, McKay?" Brandon asked.

Dylan opened the box and said, "Absolutely," as he unloaded a mountain of burgers, curly fries, and foil pillows of catsup. Next to the mountain he stood silos—the large economy-size cups—of cola. Fat and sugar, Brenda thought. Death to summer figures and clear complexions. This did not seem to be the moment to worry about such things. She dug in with the boys.

Brandon nibbled the fries and said, "These are great. Just like the ones Henry makes at your hotel."

"They *are* Henry's. He sends them over since my dad closed the suite. He knows I can't survive without my fix."

"What happened to the suite?"

Dylan shifted his position on the floor and shrugged. "Long story," he said as if he was not inclined to tell it.

"You stay here all by yourself?" Brenda asked, and then regretted it. It sounded so tacky.

But Dylan took up the challenge. He said, "Not always," and smiled lazily. He rose suddenly and swept a stack of CDs off the table. He held them out to Brenda like a magician asking a sucker to pick a card, and said, "Your turn to choose."

What Brenda wanted was not among the CDs in Dylan's hands. It wasn't a CD at all. But at the moment her choice was also her deepest secret.

Go back to the beginning...
See the 90 minutes that started it all!